Praise  W9-CID-375

BOYS IN CONTROL

"Naylor crafts a briskly paced story with a plot full of laughs
and pranks."   —*Booklist*

"A fast-paced read, and fans of the series will welcome it."
                                           —*School Library Journal*

PHYLLIS REYNOLDS NAYLOR

■ ■ ■ ■ ■ ■ ■ ■ ■

BOYS IN CONTROL

■

SCHOLASTIC INC.

New York Toronto London Auckland Sydney
Mexico City New Delhi Hong Kong Buenos Aires

ISBN-13: 978-0-545-04247-5
ISBN-10: 0-545-04247-X

Copyright © 2003 by Phyllis Reynolds Naylor. All rights reserved. Published by Scholastic Inc., 557 Broadway, New York, NY 10012, by arrangement with Random House Children's Books, a division of Random House, Inc. SCHOLASTIC and associated logos are trademarks and/or registered trademarks of Scholastic Inc. Lexile is a registered trademark of MetaMetrics, Inc.

12 11 10 9 8 7 6 5 4 3   8 9 10 11 12/0

Printed in the U.S.A.   40

First Scholastic printing, February 2008

To two of my morning pool buddies,
John Doyle and Reid Cherner,
who taught me a little something about baseball

Contents

■ ■ ■ ■ ■ ■

BOYS IN CONTROL

■ ■ ■ ■ ■ ■

One

■

Stuck

Wally Hatford took two baseball cards from his dresser—Derek Jeter and Alex Rodriguez—and stuck them in a jacket pocket. Jake had given them to him a month before just because he had duplicates, but Wally was going to trade them at school for a magic trick—a box that took a quarter and turned it into a fifty-cent piece.

When he got downstairs and hung his jacket over a chair, he found his mother moving about the kitchen and talking to herself in a state of great agitation.

"I must have been clear out of my mind!" she said, lifting the teakettle off the stove and plunking it right back down again. "I don't know what in the world possessed me to say yes last year, when I had no idea what I'd be doing a year from then."

When Mrs. Hatford talked like this, Wally and his older brothers knew to lie low. Even their father knew that as long as breakfast was on the table, it was better to sit down and butter a biscuit than to ask what she was talking about.

But Peter, who was in second grade, hadn't learned that yet. He licked the grape jelly off his fingers and asked, "What did you say yes to?"

Everyone else at the table gave him a silent shake of the head. When Mrs. Hatford started talking, it was sometimes hard to get her to stop, and the boys would be lucky to make it to school on time. But it was too late.

"The Women's Auxiliary of the Buckman Fire Department's Treats and Treasures yard sale," she said, and immediately sank down in her chair at the end of the table and rested her chin in her hands.

"Now, *that's* a mouthful," Mr. Hatford said, hiding a smile behind his mug as he finished the last of his coffee. "Did you promise to clean out our attic and look for things to give to the sale?"

"I promised to *run* the sale!" Mrs. Hatford moaned.

"At the firehouse?"

"Right here in our yard! Right out there on the driveway! Right up on our front porch!" Mrs. Hatford cried.

Now all the Hatfords were staring.

"Well, Ellen, that shouldn't be so hard," said her husband. "I'm sure the boys will help, and I'll do what I can."

2

"No, you won't, because the sale happens to be the last Saturday in May, and you know what *that* is!"

Wally tried to think, and then he remembered. That would be the day of the final game in the district elementary school baseball championships. And Jake, his brother, was on the Buckman Badgers.

"If the Badgers make it that far, you know we'll all want to be there rooting for Jake!" Mrs. Hatford said in distress. "I'm certainly going to be taking half days off from work each Saturday in May that he's playing."

Now it was a family emergency! Wally saw Jake's eyes open wide. Even Josh, Jake's twin, looked startled that his mother might have to be anywhere else on that fateful day. Jake had wanted to play for the Buckman Badgers ever since he was six years old. This was the year, and May was the month, and the twenty-ninth was the day of the championship game.

But it just so happened, Mrs. Hatford continued, that in the window of every store in town there was a poster about the Treats or Treasures yard sale, which would be held from noon till four on May twenty-ninth at the home of Tom and Ellen Hatford on College Avenue, rain or shine. So there was no getting out of it. On *that* particular day, she would need to take a *whole* day off from her job at the hardware store, but how could she be in two places at once?

There was silence around the kitchen table as sausage gravy congealed on plates and biscuits grew cold.

3

"Well, after all the practice I've put in pitching balls to Jake for the last five years, I've *got* to be at that game," said Mr. Hatford. "If I have to take four vacation days off for baseball, that's okay with me. We hadn't planned on going anywhere this summer."

"He's my twin brother! *I'm* going to be there!" said Josh.

"I've been watching Jake practice ever since I was born!" Peter declared. "I'm going to go sit in the very first row and I'll yell the loudest of all."

"Well, *I'm* Jake's *mother*!" Mrs. Hatford said. "How could I *not* be at the championship game when my very own son is one of the pitchers? At least, we *hope* the Badgers will be playing that game."

Jake scraped up some sausage gravy with his fork and put it in his mouth, looking very smug and important.

Wally knew what was coming. He knew it before the first word was spoken. He had felt that something was up the moment he'd stepped into the kitchen that morning, in fact. He wondered if he'd sensed it even before he got out of bed. And now the whole family had turned their heads and were looking down the table at him.

"No," said Wally.

"Now, Wally," said his father. "There are times when every member of a family has to stand up and be counted."

"You can count me, but I don't want to do it," said Wally.

4

"There are times you have to make sacrifices for the good of the family," said his mother. "And you have to admit that baseball isn't your favorite thing."

Wally didn't see that this made any difference. Maybe he *did* think baseball was sort of boring, and maybe he *did* like to lie back in the bleachers and study the clouds instead of watching the team practice. But did that mean he wanted to stand out on the driveway surrounded by old lamps and curtain rods and picnic hampers, arguing about prices and missing the game? The game that was going to decide the sixth-grade champion of the district?

"No!" he said again. "I don't know what any of that stuff is worth—all that stuff you'll be selling."

"Everything will have a price tag on it, Wally," his mother said.

"I can't make change!" Wally bleated. "I'm awful in math!"

"You can use my calculator," said his dad. "If you can press a button, you can make change."

"I'm only one person!" Wally wailed. "How can I look after all that stuff at once?"

"Mrs. Larson will be here to help you till the rest of us get back from the game," Mrs. Hatford said.

"Old Mrs. Larson is deaf!" Wally cried. "And she won't wear a hearing aid."

"Wait a minute, Wally. The game starts at nine in the morning and could well be over by noon," his mother told him. "The only people who will come by

5

are folks who just want to look the merchandise over. It's against the rules to sell anything before the sale opens. The other women and I will be back by noon, and if we're not, we'll be there shortly after that."

"Besides," said Josh, "if the Badgers lose any game between now and the end of May, they won't even be playing in the championship game."

"Now, that is something we're not even going to think about," said Mr. Hatford. "We're all going to think positively in the weeks ahead. Jake is going to win for the Badgers, Wally is going to do his part by keeping watch over the yard sale till Mother gets back, and then we will all help out and, hopefully, will have something to celebrate that evening."

Wally tipped his head back and closed his eyes. Why did this always happen to him? Just because he was the middle child—Peter was in second grade and the twins were in sixth—did that mean he wasn't important? Peter was the youngest, Jake and Josh the oldest, but what did that make him? Chopped liver?

"It's not fair," he wailed.

"No, it's not," said his dad, getting up and putting on his postal worker's jacket. "That's life, Wally. You win some, you lose some, and it's not always fair. But you know yourself that you are probably less interested in baseball than anyone else in this family, and all we're asking is that you miss one game in order to help your mother out."

"The *championship* game," said Wally.

6

"Yes, but we'll be as proud of you taking care of things back here as we'll be of Jake out on the pitcher's mound," said his dad.

Wally didn't say yes, but it was useless to say no because he knew when he was licked. He went upstairs to brush his teeth before school.

As he ran the brush back and forth, minty foam on his tongue, he was thinking that there was at least one other person in Buckman who felt the same way he did about baseball: Caroline Malloy. But he would have to be nailed to the wall with a gun at his head to ask Caroline to come over and help at the Treats and Treasures yard sale while his family was gone. In fact, he would have to be brain-dead to ask Caroline Malloy to come over at all.

Because whenever the Hatford kids and the Malloy kids got together, there was trouble. When Caroline and her sisters put their heads together, there was mischief you wouldn't believe.

It didn't help, of course, that Eddie Malloy was the alternate pitcher for the Buckman Badgers and that some people thought she was even better than Jake. It didn't help either that Beth would be in the bleachers cheering loudest of all for Eddie. And it especially didn't help that Caroline would undoubtedly discover Wally's absence from the championship game and would probably come looking for him, just to see what he was up to.

"I feel sick," said Wally to the mirror. Still, having

Caroline there to help might be better than not having any other helper but Mrs. Larson.

"Wally!" called his mother. "You're going to be late. Your brothers have already left for school, and the Malloy girls crossed the bridge five minutes ago."

Wally sighed and went downstairs. He pulled on his jacket and picked up his backpack. Then he went outside into the cool sunny air of a May morning, past the swinging footbridge that led across the river to the house where the Malloys were staying, and on up the street toward the school.

It used to be that his friends, the Bensons, lived in that big house on Island Avenue, where the Buckman River flowed into town on one side of the island, ran under the road bridge to the business district, then circled back out again on the other side of Island Avenue. It used to be that he and his brothers and the Benson boys spent all their time together, thinking up new things to do.

But now the Bensons had moved to Georgia for a year, the Malloys were renting their house, Jake was on the baseball team, and Wally was stuck. There was no getting around it.

Head down, shoelaces flapping, Wally trudged on up the sidewalk, reaching Buckman Elementary just as the last bell rang.

■ ■ ■ ■ ■ ■ ■ ■ ■ ■ ■

Two

■

Dreaming

Caroline Malloy pushed up her sleeves, settled back in her chair, and lifted her long dark ponytail to cool the back of her neck. Wally was going to be late if he didn't hurry. Miss Applebaum was already standing up with her roll book, looking over the class.

It wasn't that Caroline was especially fond of Wally Hatford. He certainly wasn't very fond of her, but could she help it if she was precocious and had been moved up to fourth grade? Could she help it if she had strong ambitions to be an actress, and Wally was so laid-back he just seemed to slide from one day to the next?

What she missed was being able to trace her name on the back of Wally's shirt with the edge of her ruler. Tickling him behind the ear with her pencil, and then watching his shoulders twitch and seeing first his neck, then his cheeks, then his ears turn red. Where *was* he?

9

Riiiiiing! went the last bell. A few seconds later there was the sound of running feet in the hallway and then Wally Hatford skidded into the room, stumbled down the row, and crumpled into the seat in front of Caroline.

"Well, I heard you coming, Wally, so we'll say you made it," said the teacher. "You might want to hang your jacket out there in the hall."

Wally got up, went back out the door, then came in again, a little more slowly this time.

"Good *mor*ning, Wally!" said Caroline softly, leaning forward and blowing on the back of his neck.

Wally didn't answer. He just moved sideways so that she couldn't poke him with her ruler and pretended he was listening to Miss Applebaum talk about book reports and when they were due.

Caroline sighed and folded her arms across her chest. May was going to be the most boring month if she didn't think of some way to liven it up. All the attention was going to Eddie these days—Eddie and baseball. The middle Malloy daughter, Beth, didn't seem to care if anyone paid attention to her or not. As long as Beth had a good book, especially a scary one, she was happy.

But Caroline needed attention. She loved being the main attraction, and why not? She was an actress, wasn't she, and all actresses liked an audience.

". . . a choice," Miss Applebaum was saying. "You may read a book of at least a hundred pages and write a

10

report, you may read two shorter books and compare them, or you may write a book of your own of at least ten typed pages."

Caroline's hand shot up into the air. "Could we write a play?" she asked.

Miss Applebaum looked thoughtful.

"A play is like a book. It's just mostly talking, telling what the characters are saying to each other," Caroline went on, as though her teacher did not know what a play was.

"Well, yes. I suppose it could be a play, Caroline, as long as it tells a complete story," said Miss Applebaum.

Caroline began to smile. "And will we get extra credit if we act it out for the class?"

"Yes, certainly!" said the teacher. And then she asked the class to stand for the Pledge to the flag.

"Wal-ly," Caroline whispered, moving a little closer to the boy in front of her.

"No!" Wally whispered back. "I won't be in your play."

"You don't even know what I'm going to write about," said Caroline.

"Neither do you," said Wally. "But you'll have to find someone else to do it, not me."

Caroline sighed again. It wasn't easy being a budding actress in a boring world. Still, a lot more happened here than had ever happened when she lived in Ohio. If only her family could stay here, and her dad didn't decide to move the family back again come fall.

". . . and to the Republic for which it stands," the class was saying, "one nation . . ."

I know! Caroline thought. *I'll write a mystery play, and then even Beth will read it. And if she likes it, maybe I could perform it for the whole school!*

The more Caroline thought, the more excited she became. How would you ever accomplish anything if you didn't dream? She was better at dreaming than almost anyone she knew.

There would have to be a main character, of course, with a wonderful part, and this main character would naturally be her. Maybe it would be such a good play that the newspaper would send a reporter out to review it when she performed it onstage. It might be such a great play that a talent scout would read the review and invite Caroline to audition for a part on Broadway. It might be such a brilliant play that—

"You may sit down now, Caroline," Miss Applebaum said, and there was laughter all around her. Caroline realized that the Pledge of Allegiance was long over and she was still standing. She sheepishly took her seat.

Never mind, she told herself. Someday she would be standing onstage on Broadway and everyone would be clapping. The ushers would come down the aisles carrying bouquets of roses, and she would bow to the audience—left, right, and center—and the name Caroline Lenore Malloy would be on everyone's lips as they left the theater.

When school was out for the day, most of the students went home. But those who were on the Buckman Badgers baseball team, and many of their brothers and sisters and friends, went right out to the ball field instead. The team would be practicing for the first big game of the season, coming up that Saturday. Many elementary schools had only a small field for baseball, and championship games had to be played at the local high school. But Buckman Elementary was one of the few that not only had an official ball diamond, it had bleachers as well, and on Sunday afternoons the field was open to men's amateur teams from the area.

There were sixteen sixth-grade teams competing for the championship, which meant there would be eight baseball games going on at once in different parts of the district the first Saturday in May. The eight winners would play each other the following week, the four winners would play the week after that, and on the last Saturday in May, the twenty-ninth, the two winners would play each other to see who would win the sixth-grade championship for the school district. Losing teams, however, still met at local schools to play each other, just for fun, with parents doing the coaching, so it wasn't as though you had one chance to play baseball and that was it.

But Caroline knew that Eddie had her heart set on the championship game. If the Badgers didn't make it to the finals, baseball season would be over as far as

Eddie was concerned. None of that Saturday-morning neighborhood baseball stuff for her.

Caroline had mixed feelings as she followed her two blond sisters out to the ball field behind the school. It seemed wrong to wish that Buckman would lose, and for Eddie's sake, Caroline hoped they wouldn't. But if the Badgers won the first game, and they played every Saturday in May, it would be hard to get anyone interested in her play till the games were over.

Beth, who was in fifth grade, crawled up on the bleachers beside Josh and Peter, but Caroline climbed up farther still and sat a couple of feet away from Wally Hatford, who was leaning his elbows on the riser behind him, studying a branch of the maple tree that hung out over the stands.

Wally moved a few more inches away from her, and Caroline decided right then and there that if ever she was to persuade Wally Hatford to be in a play with her, she would have to be nice to him, starting *now*.

"Hello, Wally," she said. "Nice day, isn't it?"

"We just saw each other two minutes ago," said Wally.

"So, can't I say it's a nice day anyhow?" asked Caroline.

"What do you want?" asked Wally, looking at her sideways.

"Do I have to *want* something? I just like sitting up here with you because I know you don't like baseball any more than I do," said Caroline.

"I never said I didn't like it," said Wally.

Down on the field, the coach was yelling at one of the players. "Hey, Mike! You playing baseball or chopping wood?" he called. "Don't start swinging your bat around until the pitch. You could let a ball go right past you if you're not ready."

Jake was on the pitcher's mound, and he threw a hard fastball. Sure enough, the boy in the batter's box wasn't ready. As he started his swing, the catcher had already caught the ball.

Eddie was playing shortstop in the practice game, and when the batter merely tapped the next ball, she leaped forward and caught it. Then the players changed sides and she and Jake were up to bat.

"I personally don't really care who wins the championship," Caroline said to Wally, "but Eddie and Jake will be unbearable if it's not the Buckman Badgers."

Wally shrugged. "I'm not going to be at the last game anyway, so it's no skin off my nose," he said.

"Why aren't you going to be at the game, Wally? *Every*body's going to that game if the Badgers make it that far."

"Everybody but me and Mrs. Larson," said Wally, and his voice sounded angry and disappointed.

"Where are you going with Mrs. Larson?" Caroline asked.

"I'm not going anywhere. I'm staying home. I have to be in charge of the Treats and Treasures yard sale of the Women's Auxiliary of the Buckman Fire Department the last Saturday of the month," Wally explained. "Somebody goofed and scheduled the sale the same day as the championship game, and it's already on posters all over town."

Caroline felt like laughing, but she checked herself in time and put on her most sympathetic face. "How did you get stuck with *that*?" she asked.

"Mom's making me, because everyone else in the family likes baseball more than I do. The sale's going to be in our front yard, right up on the driveway and the front porch. If the Badgers play that day, everybody will be going to that, and I have to stay home to watch over the sale stuff till the others get back."

"*I'll* help you!" said Caroline. "I don't think Eddie will miss me. I'll just come over that morning when everyone else is at the game. I'll make change or show people around or whatever you say."

Wally didn't seem to trust her, because he was still looking at her sideways. *When a person trusts you*, Caroline was thinking, *they look you right in the eye*.

"Well, okay," said Wally finally. "Maybe. If nobody else shows up to help."

And *maybe*, thought Caroline, beginning to smile, Wally had just said yes to taking a part in her play.

■ ■ ■ ■ ■ ■ ■ ■ ■ ■ ■

Three

■

Thinking Things Through

When practice was over, Wally and his brothers headed home. Wally and Peter looked somewhat alike, with round faces, brown hair, blue eyes, and thick, square hands like their father's. But the twins, Jake and Josh, had dark hair, and skin that tanned to a golden brown in summer. They were both string-bean skinny.

Usually their mother called them around three-fifteen from the hardware store where she worked to make sure they'd gotten home safely. But when they stayed for baseball practice, they called her instead.

Wally dialed the number, and as soon as his mother answered, he said, "We're all lying poisoned on the floor."

Mrs. Hatford seemed to know that meant everyone was okay because she said, "Peter didn't get his new shoes muddy, did he?"

"No, we kept him on the bleachers during practice. We didn't let him run around any."

"Good," said his mother. "You can have crackers and peanut butter, but the spaghetti is for supper, so don't touch that. The applesauce either."

"Okay," said Wally, "bye," and put the phone back down.

It used to be that as soon as the Hatfords got home from school, they would sit around the kitchen table with their afternoon snack and decide what kind of trick they were going to play next on the Malloy girls. It used to be that nothing was too awful for those girls, and the boys would do whatever they could to make them persuade their father to move them back to Ohio.

The Whomper, the Weirdo, and the Crazie, the boys called them. Eddie was the Whomper because she could hit a baseball so far—way out in center field sometimes; Beth was the Weirdo because she read such gross and scary books; and Caroline was the Crazie because she would do almost anything to be the center of attention.

But now, with Jake and Eddie on the same team, and with all the things they'd been through together, the boys had to admit that if they weren't quite friends with the Malloys, they weren't exactly enemies, either. The brothers had found themselves cheering every time Eddie made a really good play out on the field, and the Malloy girls cheered when Jake did something special.

"But if it wasn't for baseball . . . ," Jake said almost to himself, with a mouthful of crackers.

"If it wasn't for baseball, *what*?" asked Wally.

"Nothing," said Jake.

Wally seemed to know what Jake was thinking, however, because he said, "If you guys win the championship, you won't mind having Eddie around so much. You'll have your pictures in the paper and you can brag all over the place." While he spoke, Wally was fooling around with the magic trick he had traded for the two baseball cards at school. You put a quarter in one drawer, but when you pulled the drawer out a second time, the coin appeared to be gone. Then you closed it and pulled it out again and there was a fifty-cent piece in it. Except that it wasn't the same drawer. It only looked as though it was.

"And if we *don't* win?" said Jake. "What if we bomb on our very first game and then all we can play are neighborhood games for the rest of May?"

"Then . . . I don't know," said Wally, and leaned over to show Peter his trick.

"If the Bensons were here, and Steve was on our team . . . ," Jake said.

"Oh, Jake, good as he was, Steve was never as good at baseball as Eddie, and you know it," said Josh.

"Yeah, but at least if we lost out then, we'd have the guys to hang around with, do things with for the rest of the month."

"We can hang out with the girls!" Peter said helpfully.

"Eeee-yuck!" said Jake and Wally together.

"I don't need any more to do," Josh told them. "I

promised Mom I'd make signs for her Women's Auxiliary sale." He got up from the table then and went into the dining room, taking his colored markers from a drawer in the buffet. Then he reached around behind the buffet, where Mrs. Hatford stored sheets of white cardboard from the hardware store that she saved for Josh's art projects. He sat down at the table and began to make some signs.

Wally watched from the doorway. ONE TO FIVE DOLLARS Josh penciled carefully, and when the letters were straight, he went over them again with colored markers. Then he began to draw a decorative border.

Jake came and stood in the doorway too. "Hey," he said. "If we lose this weekend—if we're out of the tournament—will you guys go camping with me the rest of the weekends in May? I mean, I don't think I could *stand* losing *and* having to hang around with the Malloys."

"Sure," said Josh. "I'll go camping with you."

"Me too!" said Peter.

"Not me," said Wally. "*I* have to be here for the yard sale—" He stopped suddenly. "But if you lose, you won't be playing that day, and Mom will be here!"

"Smart boy," said Jake. "Don't go wishing we lose, though."

"Just look at it this way, Jake. No matter what happens, one of us wins," said Wally.

Jake opened his book bag and spread his homework out on the other side of the dining room table, across from Josh. Peter took a saucer of Oreo cookies into the living room to watch TV, and Wally checked the book-case to see if there were any books he hadn't read yet that he might like to read for his book report.

Hatchet he had already read. Same with *Maniac Magee*. There was another book by Jerry Spinelli he hadn't read yet, though—*Wringer*. Maybe he'd read that one.

Mr. Hatford got home from work first that day. He took off his postal jacket and hung it on a hanger. Then he went upstairs and put on a pair of sweatpants and a T-shirt. "Now, this is the kind of weather that makes me glad I'm a mail carrier," he said when he came back down. "Days like today I can drive with the window of my truck open. I can carry mail up the hill to a house, the breeze blowing at my back, and think I've got the best job in the world."

"Just the same, I don't think I want to be a mail carrier," said Wally.

"Nothing wrong with that. You can be whatever you want," said his father. "What do you want to be?"

Wally shrugged. "I just like to study things."

"What kinds of things?"

"I don't know. Just things."

His dad poured himself a glass of cold tea from a pitcher, then put the pitcher back in the refrigerator. "Well, you could be a biologist and study cells under a microscope."

"Maybe," said Wally.

"You could be a zoologist and study animals."

"That'd be okay," said Wally.

"Or you could be a sociologist and study people."

"I'll stick with animals," said Wally. He settled down in one corner of the couch to start reading *Wringer*. It was about a town in Pennsylvania where there was a pigeon shoot every year to raise money, and boys about Wally's age worked at grabbing any pigeons that were shot but not dead yet, and wringing their necks, and this one boy didn't want to do it.

I wouldn't want to do it either, thought Wally. *What kind of a person would want to twist the head off a pigeon?* Maybe he *should* study people after all.

When Mrs. Hatford came home, she found all the members of her family busy. After checking on everyone in turn, she set about making supper, humming to herself.

"I feel so much better knowing you will be here to look after things at the sale, Wally," she said when he came in to see if the food was ready yet.

And I feel so much worse, thought Wally.

After supper he took his book bag up to his room to work on his math assignment. He was surprised to find two boxes, a lampshade, and a framed picture in one corner. He went to the top of the stairs.

"Hey!" he yelled. "What's that stuff doing in my room?"

His mother came to the foot of the stairs. "Oh, I hope you don't mind, Wally. We've told all the women not to bring their sale items to the house until the day before the sale, but some of them will be out of town then, and others just want them out of the way. Better to have them early than not at all, I guess."

"But what are they doing in *my* room?" Wally bellowed.

"Well, I looked in the twins' bedroom, and they've got so much stuff in there, and so does Peter, that—"

"What about the *basement*?" Wally wailed.

"Things might get musty down there, dear. Be a good sport, please, Wally. It's only till the end of the month, I promise."

Wally went back into his room and lay facedown on the bed. Just because he kept his room neat—just because he put things back in the right place—did he have to be punished? If he were a slob like Josh or Jake or Peter, would she have put the sale stuff somewhere else? Or did the middle child get the worst of everything? Wouldn't want to store stuff in the twins' bedroom because they're the oldest. Wouldn't want to put it in Peter's room. He's the youngest. So good old Wally—

The phone rang and he heard Jake answer at the foot of the stairs.

"Oh, hi, Eddie." Jake's voice was flat. ". . . No, I don't think so. I've got too much to do. . . . Yeah, bye."

Wally got up and went downstairs. "What did *she* want?" he asked, curious.

"Wanted to know if I would go over to the school and get in some extra practice. I told her no."

"How come?" asked Wally.

"Because Eddie doesn't *need* more practice. If I help her get even better, Coach'll let her pitch *all* the games. What kind of a fool does she take me for?"

"But you'd get better too!" said Wally.

The phone rang again. This time Wally picked it up.

"Is this the Hatford residence?" came a woman's voice.

"Yes," said Wally.

"I understand you are collecting things for the Women's Auxiliary sale on May twenty-ninth?"

"Yes," said Wally.

"I was wondering if I might come by early and look over what you've collected so far, and make a purchase."

"I don't think so, but I'll ask," said Wally.

He went to the kitchen and asked his mother. When he came back, he said, "No, we can't sell anything before the sale opens at noon on that day, but if you'll give me your name and phone number—"

The phone at the other end clicked as the woman hung up.

Four

■

Out!

"Jake Hatford is a jerk!"

Eddie Malloy stood in the upstairs hallway, phone in hand, before plunking it disgustedly down in its cradle.

"What now?" asked Beth from her bedroom.

"All I did was ask if he wanted to go back to the school later and get in some practice, and he said no."

Caroline followed Eddie into Beth's room.

"Maybe he had homework," Beth suggested, putting her finger between the pages of her book to hold the place.

"It was just an excuse, I could tell," said Eddie. "Doesn't he want to get any better before Saturday?"

"Maybe he just doesn't want to see *you* get any better," said Beth.

"That's ridiculous! We're on the same team!" Eddie fumed. "Doesn't he want us to *win*?"

"Not as bad as he wants to see you *not* win," said Beth.

"I will never understand boys as long as I live," said Eddie. "They were all born with half a brain."

"Peter's cute," said Caroline.

"Cute won't cut it," said Eddie.

"Josh is nice at times," said Beth.

"If you like the arty type," said Eddie.

Beth and Caroline exchanged glances.

"And what type do *you* like, Eddie? The sports type?" giggled Beth. "Maybe you thought Jake would jump at the chance to go over to the school with you alone, and he didn't. Maybe *that's* why you think he's a jerk."

"Give me a break," Eddie said. She turned on her heels, walked into her room, and shut the door.

Caroline sat down on the floor and leaned back against the wall. "What kind of book are you reading?" she asked.

"Mystery," said Beth.

"That's your favorite kind, isn't it? Scary stories?"

"Mystery and science fiction and romance—those are my three favorites," said Beth.

Caroline thought about that a moment. "If someone gave you a play that had mystery and romance and science fiction in it, all mixed up together, would you read it?"

"Whose play?"

"Mine," said Caroline.

"No," said Beth.

"Why not? Miss Applebaum said I could write a ten-page play instead of a book report, and if I can get it performed in front of the class, I'll get extra credit."

"Well, don't look at me. I'm not going to be in your play. I'm not getting up there on the stage at school and making a fool of myself."

"All I want you to do is read it when I'm done and tell me if it's any good," said Caroline.

"Sure," said Beth. "Now go away and let me finish my book."

■

It rained on Wednesday and Thursday, and the ground was still too wet for practice on Friday, so when the time came on Saturday, Eddie had been without practice and was feeling nervous.

Caroline had never seen her sister so jumpy. Usually Eddie was pretty much in control, but by the time the Malloys pulled into the parking lot of the high school in Elkins, where the game would be played, she was nibbling at her lower lip and looking tense.

"What's the matter, Eddie?" Caroline whispered.

"I don't know. I'm just jittery," Eddie confessed. She was sitting between her two sisters in the backseat, and kept taking deep breaths. "I feel rusty without practice."

"I don't know why you should be nervous," said Beth. "You're better than almost any boy on the team, and no one else got in extra practice either."

"But you know what will happen if we lose," said

Eddie. "Especially if we lose our first game. They'll blame it on me. They'll say it's because there's a girl on the team. And nobody will ever want to talk to me at school."

"Eddie, that's ridiculous," said her father. "You know what? You're a lot more nervous sitting here in the car thinking about how you'll play than you'll be when you're actually out there on the field." He turned off the engine. "Okay, girl. Go!" he said.

The Malloys piled out just as the Hatfords were getting out of their car. Peter was squeezed between his parents in front. Caroline studied the Hatford boys. Jake didn't look nervous at all. The Hatfords looked in control of the situation. Jake, in fact, looked as though he could handle anything. There was a swagger to his walk as he sauntered over to survey the other team, which was warming up out on the field.

Parents and friends took their places on the bleachers, Elkins parents on one end, Buckman parents on the other. There was an empty space, a no-man's-land, in between.

The Hatfords sat in front of the Malloys, and as soon as they were seated, Peter turned around and said, "Jake's gonna strike everybody out!" The others laughed.

"We'll see what happens, Peter. We'll see," said his dad.

The other team was at bat, and Eddie was the starting pitcher. But Caroline could tell just by her windup that she was off her stride. The ball didn't come as fast as it usually did, and the first batter hit it to center field. Fortunately for Buckman, it was caught. One out.

The next batter walked. The third batter hit a double, and the runner on first scored. By the time the first inning was over, Elkins had one run, Buckman, nothing.

The coach was talking to Eddie and Jake. And Caroline knew without hearing that Jake would pitch the second inning. While Eddie was waiting her turn at bat, she paced behind the catcher like a tiger. *Nibble, nibble, nibble* went her teeth on her lower lip.

"What do you suppose is wrong with her?" Mrs. Malloy asked her husband.

"Just the first time she's played on a real team," her husband answered. "No matter how much practice you get, there's always that first time." Mr. Malloy was a football coach at Buckman College. He was replacing Coach Benson for a year on a teacher-exchange program. Whether he would take his family back to Ohio when the year was over or stay in Buckman had not yet been decided.

Buckman struck out before Eddie got a chance to bat. When the Badgers took the field again, the coach put Eddie in left field and Jake on the pitcher's mound. Jake struck out two batters and got the third out on a weak infield fly.

When Buckman's players came to bat, Eddie was batting third. The first boy struck out. The second batter made it to first when the shortstop fumbled the ball. When Eddie got up, Mr. Malloy murmured to Caroline, "She's leaning too far forward." Eddie swung and missed.

"Strike one!" called the umpire.

Eddie didn't swing at the second pitch.

"Strike two!" the umpire said.

Eddie lifted the bat slightly off her shoulder. The Elkins pitcher wound up and threw the ball. Eddie swung.

Craaaaack! Eddie, surprised that she had actually hit the ball, let go of the bat as she started to run to first. The next thing anyone knew, the bat had traveled down the line of Buckman players waiting their turn and hit two of them across the knees.

The umpire stopped play.

"You're out of the game, Eddie," he yelled. "She's out of the game, Coach, for throwing her bat."

Down on the field, Eddie looked stricken. Dazed. "I . . . I didn't mean to," she kept saying.

Her coach shook his head. "You know the rules, Eddie. You never let go of the bat like that. You could have hit a player in the face. Go sit on the bench."

Beth covered her face with her hands, but Caroline couldn't take her eyes off her older sister. Seemingly in shock, Eddie went slowly back to the bench and sat down, her face blank.

The game continued without her. Jake had never played better. He was in control of his arm and his arm was in control of the ball. Buckman tied the score, then got a run in the eighth inning. No one scored in the ninth, so Buckman advanced to the next game the following Saturday. The team was greeted with cheers as they picked up their bats and balls to go home.

Eddie didn't say a word as she followed her family across the parking lot to the car. Coach Malloy reached out and put an arm around her shoulder, but Eddie didn't respond. It was only when they were inside the car that she said shakily, "I don't know what was the matter, Dad! I just blew it, that's all. I've never thrown a bat like that, ever!"

"And I don't think you will again, Eddie," said her father.

"I just felt like . . . like everyone was looking at me, expecting great things, and that no matter how well I played, it wouldn't be good enough," she said miserably.

Coach Malloy smiled a little. "Well, by next week, word will get around that you aren't very good after all, and nobody will expect much of anything. And *then* you can show them what you can do."

Eddie sat with her head down. "This is so humiliating!" she murmured. "Jake didn't seem nervous at all. He's going to hate me for letting the team down."

"Oh, I don't think so," said her dad. "The Badgers won, didn't they? Show up every day for practice, Eddie, and do your best."

The girls went upstairs as soon as they got home,

and Eddie seemed too tired even to talk. She certainly didn't want any lunch. When the phone rang, Caroline took it in the upstairs hall. It was Jake.

"Can I talk to Eddie?" he said.

"Eddie," Caroline called. "For you. It's Jake."

"I don't want to talk to him," said Eddie. "Tell him I'm sick or something."

"I guess she's too tired," said Caroline into the phone.

There was a pause at the end of the line. "Well, tell her I'm going over to the school this afternoon and get in some practice, and I wondered if she wanted to come along," said Jake.

"Just a minute," said Caroline. She walked to the door of Eddie's bedroom and told her what Jake had said.

Eddie was quiet for a moment. "Yes," she said finally. "Tell him I'd like that."

■ ■ ■ ■ ■ ■ ■ ■ ■ ■ ■

Five

■

Act One

When Jake set off for the school ball field that afternoon, he told his brothers to stay home.

"Eddie doesn't need to have people staring at her,"
he said. "She feels bad enough already."

Wally could only stare at Jake. It seemed to Wally that
while Eddie had lost her self-confidence, Jake seemed to
have found his. Now that Eddie had proved she wasn't
so hot, wasn't superhuman, Jake could shine. And once
he shone, he didn't have to dislike Eddie so much.

"We need her on the team," Jake said to his brothers.
"If she doesn't play any better than she did this morning, we'll lose." He went outside and down the street
toward the school.

Wally decided to spend the afternoon reading
Wringer for his book report, but he was almost afraid to
go in his bedroom anymore. It seemed as though every
time he left, the bags and boxes along the wall had

babies. All he had to do was leave the house for an hour or two and when he came back there would be another lampshade or Crock-Pot or toaster.

"Just hold on till the end of the month, Wally, and you'll have your room back the way it was," said his mother.

"What if some of this stuff doesn't sell?" he asked.

"Mrs. Larson's son has promised to haul away to the Goodwill store anything that's left," his mother said.

It was a beautiful spring day, so Wally decided he would rather read outside than in his room anyway. He went out on the back steps with a glass of lemonade and his book and tried to think how much lemon juice and water it took to make a pitcher of lemonade. And once he started thinking about water, he thought about how much rain they had had that spring. Once he started thinking about what a rainy spring it had been, he started to remember the year before, when it had hardly rained at all and farmers had worried about drought. The newspaper had asked people to take fewer baths and shorter showers. They were told not to water their lawns and to make sure their dishwashers were full before they turned them on.

Here's what Wally could not understand: If the water from your sink and your bathtub went into the sewer, and the sewers flowed into rivers, and the water you drank came from the river, through filtration plants, and then back on into your house, what difference did it make if you used too much bathwater or not? Didn't it just end up in the river again? He knew there must be a good reason, but no one had ever explained it to him.

He had taken another sip of lemonade when he saw Caroline coming up his driveway. He tried to pull his feet out of the way so that she wouldn't know he was out back, but it was too late. Around the house she came. She was holding a writing tablet and pencil.

"Hi, Wally," she said. "I guess Jake and Eddie are over at the school practicing, aren't they?"

"I guess so," said Wally.

"Eddie was pretty upset over the way she played this morning. Jake was nice to offer to practice with her."

"I guess so," said Wally again, studying the slice of lemon in his glass.

"I brought over the first act of my play, Wally. Can I read it to you for your frank and honest opinion?"

"I guess so," said Wally.

Caroline studied him. "You have to be one hundred percent honest or it won't help," she said. "When I get to be an actress on Broadway, critics will come to see me perform and the newspapers will publish their reviews. I have to get used to criticism, so say whatever you really feel about it. Okay?"

"Okay," said Wally.

Caroline cleared her throat, held the tablet out in front of her, and began: "A Night to Forget," she read. "Act one, scene one: A cottage on the beach. Ten o'clock at night. A couple is on their honeymoon."

JIM: Wasn't that a nice walk on the beach, honey?

NANCY: Yes, it was. And wasn't the moon beautiful?

JIM: Yes, it was.

NANCY: I wonder what those strange marks were on the sand, though.

JIM: Probably just a crab or some sort of seagull.

NANCY: I suppose so. *She yawns.*

JIM: Well, I guess we should go to bed.

NANCY: Yes, I'm very tired.

JIM: I'll turn out the lights.

NANCY: Wait a minute. What was that noise? It sounds like something trying to get in.

JIM: Probably just the wind. I think you're imagining things.

NANCY: I suppose so. Good night.

JIM: Good night.

They kiss.

Wally found Caroline looking at him. He also felt his neck beginning to get red.

"Okay so far?" asked Caroline.

"I guess so," said Wally.

"Act one, scene two," said Caroline. "Twelve o'clock at night. Jim and Nancy's bedroom. There is just enough moonlight coming in the window that the audience can see what's onstage."

NANCY: Jim! Jim! Wake up. I hear that noise again.

JIM: Huh?

NANCY: I hear it, and it's louder now! I really think someone's trying to get in.

JIM: But we're the only ones on the beach. There aren't any other houses for miles around. Who would it be?

NANCY: I don't know, but I think you should do something.

JIM: Okay. I hear it now too. I'll go downstairs and check.

There is a sloshing, thumping, scraping noise offstage.

NANCY: Oh, Jim! Be careful!

JIM: Don't fear, my love. I'll be okay.

Nancy sits up in bed with one hand to her throat. Jim grabs a golf club and goes out into the hall in his pajamas. The noise gets louder and louder, and then there is a terrible yell from Jim.

NANCY: Jim! Jim!

There is a gurgling sound from downstairs and then the house is quiet. Nancy leaps out of bed and backs up against the wall, her eyes wide. When Jim does not come back, she runs over and locks the bedroom door and then she gets back in bed. Soon she is sound asleep.

"What?" said Wally. "Her husband disappears and she just goes back to sleep?"

Caroline thoughtfully tapped her pencil against her cheek. "Okay," she said. "She'll lie there with her eyes wide open until morning." Caroline made a note on her tablet, then began reading aloud again:

Act one, scene three: Morning in the cottage. Nancy sits up in bed sobbing.

NANCY: Jim! Jim! Where are you? *There is no answer. She gets out of bed and looks out the window. The sky is dark and brooding.*

NANCY: I know! I'll call the beach patrol. They will come over and help us. *She lifts up the telephone.* Oh, no! The line is dead!

She puts on her robe and combs her hair. Then she takes another one of her husband's golf clubs and carefully opens the bedroom door.

NANCY: Jim? Jim?

She takes a step outside into the hall.

NANCY: Jim? Jim?

No answer. She screams. She puts her hands to her face. She screams again. She bends down and touches something on the floor. The floor and the stairs are covered with a thick green slime. Curtain falls. End of act one.

Caroline closed her writing tablet and looked at Wally. "Well," she said, "how did you like it?"

"It stinks," said Wally.

"What?" cried Caroline.

"You wanted me to be truthful," said Wally.

"But you have to say more than 'It stinks,' " said Caroline. "This play has everything! It has romance and science fiction and suspense and mystery!"

"It still stinks," said Wally. And then, thinking that perhaps he sounded a bit harsh, he said, "Of course, I've only heard the first act. I probably shouldn't say anything until I've heard it all."

"Right," said Caroline. "But what's the matter with it so far?"

Wally shrugged. "They don't sound like real people. Why didn't the wife call the beach patrol before? Why did she wait till morning?"

Caroline thought about that a moment. "Because I wanted her to discover that the line was dead at the end of act one, and that would be the next morning."

"Well, why wouldn't she go downstairs as soon as she heard her husband scream, then?"

"Because I'm saving that for act two," said Caroline.

"Well," said Wally. "Like I said, so far it stinks, but maybe the next act will be better."

Caroline sighed. "Maybe I'm a better actress than I am a playwright. But I wanted to write a play with a part especially for me."

"So does Nancy die a horrible death in the end? That would be a good part for you," said Wally.

"I can't give away the ending," said Caroline.

"Who's going to play the part of Jim?" asked Wally, and when Caroline just looked at him and smiled, he said, "No!"

"That's okay," said Caroline. "When I've finished it, it will be so good that every boy in school will want to play the part of Jim."

"Name one," said Wally.

Caroline thought some more. "Well, Peter, maybe."

Wally laughed out loud, and Caroline smiled a little too. "Just wait, Wally," she said. "Someday you will see my name in lights on Broadway and you'll be proud to say you knew me when I was just a little girl."

■ ■ ■ ■ ■ ■ ■ ■ ■ ■

Six

■

Scavenger Hunt

"**G**irls," Mrs. Malloy called up the stairs when the girls got home from school the following Wednesday. "When you finish your homework, will you take a half hour or so to check your rooms and see if you have anything—any *nice* thing—that we could donate to Ellen Hatford for the yard sale?"

"Like what?" asked Eddie.

"Oh, maybe a shirt you haven't worn much. Belts, jewelry, anything at all that might catch someone's eye. I've put a box in the hall up there for your things. But don't give away anything with holes in it. We'll put things like that in the rag bag, and I can use them around the house."

Eddie was the most generous when it came to give-aways. She stood at her closet door, sliding hangers from left to right. For each item she said either a soft yes or no. A yes meant it could be given away, and she would yank it off the hanger and throw it onto her bed. A no meant it was a keeper. To Caroline, it seemed as though Eddie had no second thoughts. No sentimental attachments. And when she had finished her closet, she started on her dresser drawers.

Beth was more of a problem, especially with books. Asking Beth to get rid of a book was about like asking Mrs. Malloy to get rid of a daughter. But Caroline was the absolute worst, and she knew it. Caroline, it seemed, could get rid of nothing, because every object, every item of clothing, every old sneaker, in fact, was something that she might, someday, in middle school or high school, be able to use as a prop in a play. It might be just the right necklace for the part, or the right music box, or even the perfect moth-eaten sweater for an orphaned child to wear onstage. When Mrs. Malloy came upstairs later to see how the girls were doing, she found a box full of Eddie's things, only a jacket from Beth, and nothing at all from Caroline.

Caroline sat on her bed, surrounded by things her mother thought she'd parted with years before, misty-eyed and clutching each one to her in turn.

"Good grief," said Mrs. Malloy. "I'm not asking you to sacrifice body parts, Caroline. If you haven't made use of something since first grade, let it go, for heaven's sake."

And so a little doll in a Swiss costume was donated to the sale, a *Bambi* video, a pair of patent leather shoes that were a size too small, and a wool cap.

"We're not supposed to take things over to the Hatfords' yet, so we'll keep them here until the night before the sale," Mrs. Malloy said. "But this will save us some work later if we move back to Ohio."

"*Will* we go back, Mother?" Beth asked.

"I wish I knew! One day your father thinks he'll stay on here for another year as football coach and the next he doesn't. It will depend partly on whether Coach Benson decides to move *his* family back from Georgia and take over their house. It's like dominoes. Everyone's waiting for the next piece to fall."

■

"Well, I feel great!" Eddie announced at supper. "I've done well at practice every day this week, and I don't think I'll be too nervous at Saturday's game. I was afraid the coach would take me off the team after last week, but he says no way. Just a question of the first-game jitters, he calls it."

"That's the spirit, Eddie!" said her father. "Where's the next game? Clarksburg, is it?"

"Yeah. Are you coming?"

"Wouldn't miss it for the world," Coach Malloy said.

■

At school, the kids in Caroline's class were beginning to read their book reports aloud. Every day in English two or three more students got up to tell why they had chosen a particular book.

Wally stood up and read his report about *Wringer*. Everyone listened intently, especially when they found out there really *was* such a town in Pennsylvania, and that there really *was* a pigeon shoot, and that boys really *were* hired to wring the necks of injured and dying pigeons.

"Very good, Wally," the teacher said. "Isn't it interesting how Mr. Spinelli took an incident from real life and turned it into a work of fiction?"

At recess, when people were putting their books away, Caroline said to Wally, "I think that sounds like a good book. It's sad, but I'll read it sometime."

"I didn't do a good job telling about it, though," said Wally. "There's a lot of stuff going on in the book that just doesn't come out in a report."

"Just like my play!" said Caroline. "I could see all kinds of things going on in my head while I was reading it that you couldn't see when you heard it. That's what actors and actresses do—they bring the words to life onstage."

Wally thought about that a minute. "Well, maybe," he said. "Maybe I'll like the second act better."

■

There was, of course, baseball practice again after school, and when the Malloy girls finally got home and were sharing a bag of chips, they noticed more bags and boxes in the hall.

"What's this?" Beth asked her mother.

"More things for the Women's Auxiliary sale," said Mrs. Malloy. "This is giving us a chance to clean house. When you girls finish your snack, would you go down in the basement and see if there's anything else that could go?"

"Most of that stuff belongs to the Bensons," said Eddie.

"I know. But we put some of our own things down there too."

So the girls sauntered over to the basement door and went down the steps. Eddie and Caroline rummaged through the old tires and garden hoses along one wall, while Beth stood back on the stairs, surveying the basement and holding the bag of chips.

Suddenly Beth said, "Hey!"

Eddie and Caroline turned around.

"What?" asked Caroline.

Beth stuffed another handful of chips in her mouth and pointed to the long metal heating ducts overhead.

"*What?*" said Eddie, and went back up the stairs to where Beth was standing, to see where she was pointing.

There, on top of a metal duct, almost out of sight, was a small notebook or something.

"What do you think it is?" asked Beth, still chewing.

"I don't know," Eddie said. "Furnace instructions maybe?" She went back down the steps, pulled the stepladder over, then climbed up and ran her hand over the top of the metal duct until she reached the notebook. She pulled it down and a shower of plaster dust and dirt came with it.

"Yuck!" she said, lowering her head and flicking the stuff from her hair.

It was a small photo album with no label on the cover. Still standing on the ladder, Eddie opened it up. Her eyes grew wide and a slow smile spread across her face. "Hey!" she said. "Pay dirt!"

"What is it?" asked Caroline, reaching for it. But Eddie only clutched it to her chest, came back down the ladder, and, grinning mysteriously, motioned her sisters to follow her up to her room.

"Find anything for the sale?" Mrs. Malloy called from the dining room.

"Only old tires, and those are the Bensons'," Eddie answered.

Up in her room, Eddie closed the door behind them and the three girls sprawled on her bed.

"You'll never guess!" Eddie said, still smiling, and opened the cover. There were color photographs of . . . who else? The Hatford and Benson boys, in the silliest pictures the girls had ever seen. They appeared to have been taken sometime in the past year, for the boys looked only a little younger than they were now.

Yet there was Peter Hatford dressed in a diaper, curled up on a blanket and sucking a bottle. There was Jake with strands of cooked spaghetti dangling from his nostrils, a cap with a propeller on his head. There was Wally in bunny pajamas two sizes too small, with sleeper feet and floppy ears. There was Josh in Batman underpants and a Batman T-shirt with a cape around his shoulders.

The girls were too astonished to make a sound at first; then they burst into laughter at the humiliating pictures of the boys. The five Benson brothers had their photos in the album too: Steve Benson dressed as a ballerina; Bill bending over with a rip in the seat of his pants, blowing soap bubbles at the same time; Tony in white knee socks with a pacifier in his mouth and a Dr. Seuss hat on his head; Doug holding a teddy bear and sucking his thumb; and Danny wearing a T-shirt that said KICK ME HARD, holding a blueberry pie in which he had obviously just buried his face.

"What do you suppose made them take these pictures?" Eddie gasped in disbelief.

"I don't know," said Beth, "but this is too good to pass up." She went to the phone in the hallway and dialed the Hatfords' number.

Wally answered, and Beth held the phone out so that her sisters could hear.

"Hi, Wally, this is Beth," she said. "I just wanted to tell you that I think we've found something else for your Treats and Treasures yard sale."

"Good," said Wally. "Bring it over on the twenty-eighth, okay?"

"Oh, but I thought you should know about it first," Beth went on. "We found it in the basement on top of a heating duct."

"Yeah?" said Wally.

"It's a photo album, with pictures."

"Yeah?" Wally said again.

"And you look really great in those bunny pajamas," Caroline said over Beth's shoulder, giggling.

"What?" yelled Wally, and the girls heard him bellow, "Josh! They found those pictures!"

Josh's voice sounded from the kitchen. "Who did? What pictures?"

"The Malloys. The *pictures*!" he squawked.

There were cries of anguish in the background; then Josh took the phone. "Where were they?" he asked, his voice tense.

"On top of a heating duct in the basement," Beth explained. "We thought we'd offer them for the Women's Auxiliary yard sale. Unless, of course, you guys want to negotiate or make a trade of some sort."

"Trade for *what*?" asked Josh.

"I don't know, we'll think of something," Beth said, and hung up, still laughing.

Seven

■

Missing

Josh threw back his head and howled, Jake and Wally joining in.

Mrs. Hatford was just coming through the back door, and she paused as she dropped her car keys on the counter.

"Is this a braying contest or something?"

"That stupid Bill Benson!" Wally cried.

"Stupid Steve and Tony and all of them! They should have taken those pictures with them!" said Josh.

"What on earth are you talking about?" asked their mother.

Josh look at Jake and Jake looked at Wally and nobody wanted to say anything, but finally Peter, the only one who seemed calm, spoke up: "Pictures," he said.

"Pictures of whom?"

"Us," said Peter.

"So?" said his mother.

"Doing silly things," Peter answered uncertainly, looking at his brothers for guidance.

"Well, is that so awful? What kinds of things?" asked Mrs. Hatford as she went to the refrigerator to see what to make for dinner. She took out a package of pork chops and studied the lower shelf.

Josh did the telling. After all, Wally figured, he was making all those beautifully decorated signs for the yard sale. His mother could hardly get mad at him.

"Jake had spaghetti coming out of his nose," he said.

Mrs. Hatford straightened up and looked around. "He had *what*?"

"And I was wearing a diaper and sucking on a bottle!" Peter said, laughing.

Mrs. Hatford turned slowly to Wally.

"I was wearing my old bunny pajamas and Josh was in his Batman underpants and a cape."

Mrs. Hatford was trying not to laugh. "*Why* would you guys want your pictures taken like *that*?"

"The Bensons did it too!" said Peter. "One of 'em was in a ballerina costume and one put his face in a blueberry pie and—"

"*Why?*" Mrs. Hatford asked again.

The boys looked at each other.

"Just for fun," Josh said finally.

"So where are they?"

"The Malloys found them in the basement."

"Well, for goodness' sake, just ask the girls to give them back!" said Mrs. Hatford. "Now, let me see if we have any more applesauce in the cellar." And she went down the stairs.

The boys looked at each other. There were times, Wally thought, when their mother seemed to be the smartest woman in the world and times, like now, when she seemed to have no imagination whatsoever. Did she really think that the girls, who had thought of every trick in the book to play on them—girls, in fact, whom the boys had tormented from the very moment they moved to Buckman—were going to give back pictures of the boys in their underpants and bunny pajamas? Did she really believe that if Wally went over to the Malloys' house and said, "Could you please let us have those ridiculous pictures back, the ones with spaghetti coming out of Jake's nose?" the girls would say "Sure," and hand them over? Was she living on another planet?

They went up to the twins' bedroom to think it over.

"Why did we ever take those pictures in the first place?" Wally wondered aloud.

"You know why, Wally!" said Josh. "We were all in on it. We made a pact that we would always be loyal to each other, no matter what, and to make sure, we took the most embarrassing picture we could think of for each one of us. If one of us ever betrayed the rest, we were going to show his picture around school."

"Oh, yeah." Wally sighed. "It seemed like a good idea at the time."

"Until the dumb, stupid Bensons forgot to take the

pictures with them!" said Jake. "Just tell me this, Wally. Was Eddie on the phone? Was she doing any of the talking?"

"No. Only Beth," said Wally.

"Well, maybe Eddie didn't see the pictures, then," said Jake. "She might get them back for us, now that we're working together on the same team."

"And maybe pigs have wings," said Josh.

"Well, I'm not going to get upset before this next game!" Jake declared. "I'm not even going to think about it, if I can help it. Josh, you'll have to bargain with them."

"How?" Josh bleated. "The only Malloy who likes me a little is Beth, and it was Beth who was doing the talking!"

All eyes turned to Wally. "No!" said Wally. Then he shouted it. *"NO!"*

This time they must have taken him seriously, because suddenly the twins turned toward Peter.

"Peter," said Josh. "We really, really need you. We need you to go over to the Malloys' and ask for those pictures. Just get those pictures and bring them back. And don't come home until you do."

"Okay," said Peter. He went back downstairs and out the door.

Wally looked at his brothers. This was too easy. They stood at the window at the top of the stairs and watched the youngest Hatford go down the walk and cross the road. They watched him start across the swinging bridge. When he got to the center, where the supporting cables on each side hung low enough to grab as handrails, they watched him stop and peer over the edge.

"Why is he just standing there?" Jake asked. "What's he *doing*?"

"Spitting," said Wally.

"What?"

"That's what he's doing," said Wally. "He's spitting in the water to see how far it will float."

Jake and Josh stared at Wally.

"You can't see your own spit in the water. It gets mixed up with the river."

"I know," said Wally. "But that's what Peter's trying to find out."

His brothers were still looking at Wally strangely, though, and Wally wondered if he and Peter were the only boys in Upshur County who had ever passed a May afternoon by spitting in the Buckman River.

Eventually, however, Peter began walking forward again, stopping now and then to try to see the river between the slats in the bridge, and at long last he reached the other side and started up the Malloys' hilly lot.

"I sure didn't need this right now," said Jake. "I'm trying not to let *any*thing throw me off stride for Saturday's game. Clarksburg's going to be a tough team to beat."

"Well, I sure didn't need it either," said Josh. "What

if Beth brings those pictures to school and puts one up on the bulletin board or something?"

It went without saying that Wally didn't need this either. He didn't need it now or ever. He didn't need Caroline sticking the picture of him in his bunny pajamas on the end of a ruler and thrusting it over his shoulder at school. He didn't need her passing the pictures around the girls' table at lunch. He didn't need to walk by groups of giggling girls out on the playground and see them all point to him. No sir, he didn't need that at all.

"Do you think they'll give the album to him?" Josh asked as the minutes ticked by and Peter disappeared from view at the top of the hill.

"If they give the pictures to anyone, it will be Peter," said Jake. "They like Peter. They think he's just the sweetest thing that ever lived. Ha! They should check out his closet sometime. They should smell his breath after he's eaten cheese! But hey! If Peter gets the pictures back, he can smell like dog doo for all I care."

Mr. Hatford's car turned into the driveway, and the boys could hear his footsteps as he came into the house.

They heard the voices of their parents in the kitchen below, and the sound of the TV as Mr. Hatford turned on the evening news. There came the smell of frying pork chops, and the clatter of plates on the table.

Wally and his brothers stood at the upstairs window, noses pressed against the glass.

"Come . . . on!" Josh breathed.

"Where *is* he?" said Jake.

"Well, you can't expect him just to say, 'Give me the pictures,' and think they'll hand them right over," said Wally. "He's got to be sweet first."

"Man, I don't know how he does it. He's so sweet that the girls always feed him cookies when he goes over there," said Jake.

"They *bake* them especially for him," said Josh.

"Which makes him even sweeter," said Wally.

Five more minutes went by. Then ten.

"Boys!" came their mother's voice from below. "Wash up. Supper's on the table."

"Oh, man!" Wally whispered.

"Coming!" called Josh.

They went into the bathroom and washed their hands, doing everything in slow motion, hoping to stall for time.

Down the stairs they went, stopping at the front door to peer out again at the swinging bridge, looking for a lone figure coming down the hill from the Malloys' with a photo album under his arm.

Nothing.

They went into the kitchen, where mashed potatoes and green beans and pork chops sat on various platters, and a dish of applesauce stood in the center of the table.

Mrs. Hatford glanced around at her brood, then went to the kitchen doorway and called, "Peter?"

"Uh . . . he'll be back any minute, Mom," said Wally. "He's doing an errand."

"At suppertime?" his mother asked.

"He'll be along," Josh echoed.

The rolls in the oven were just beginning to brown around the edges, and Mrs. Hatford grabbed the pot holders to take them out. For the next few minutes she was busy with that. The boys helped themselves to the food at hand and amiably discussed the rolls and how good they were spread with their mother's cherry jam.

But right in the middle of supper, Mrs. Hatford said, "Where *is* Peter? Where did he go?"

"He should have been back by now," said Wally.

"Do you or do you not know where he went?" asked Mr. Hatford.

"He went to the Malloys' to get some pictures back," said Josh.

"Aha! So he's doing the dirty work for you," said Mrs. Hatford. "How long ago did he leave?"

"Twenty minutes, maybe," said Jake.

"Say thirty," said Josh.

"Well, for heaven's sake, he should have been back by now," said Mrs. Hatford, looking concerned.

And at that very moment the phone rang.

Eight

■

The Visitor

"Who do you suppose will come over to get it?" Beth asked mischievously.

"I don't know, but I'm going to let you two handle it," said Eddie. "Jake and I are getting along okay right now, and I don't want any trouble between us before the game on Saturday. He was awfully nice to practice with me last week, so if there's any negotiating to do, you guys will have to do it."

"Man oh man, do we ever hold all the cards!" said Beth. "We've never been in such a good bargaining position before, Caroline. What should we ask for in return? All their earthly possessions?"

"We'd better think about this a long time," said Caroline. "We don't want to blow it. Maybe we shouldn't decide until the championship game is over. We could tell the guys we'll give it back in June, and we'll make our conditions then."

"Good idea," said Eddie. "We're not saying we won't give it back. We're just saying we won't give it back right now."

"Let's take another look at it," said Beth. "I want to imprint these on my brain forever." She giggled.

The girls sat down on the bed again, and this time they savored every picture. They hooted and howled when they came to the photo of Wally Hatford in bunny pajamas two sizes too small, and Caroline even rolled off the bed in laughter.

There was a knock at the door downstairs, and Caroline continued rolling till she was on her feet again and was the first one to reach the door. There stood Peter, smiling his sweetest smile.

"Well, hello, Peter." Caroline grinned at him, then turned around and grinned at her sisters on the stairs. "Want to come in?" she asked him.

"Okay," said Peter, and stepped into the hallway.

"Who is it?" called Coach Malloy from the kitchen, where he was helping cut up vegetables for dinner.

"Just Peter Hatford, over for a little visit," Beth called back.

Peter came in and sat in a chair in a corner of the living room.

"How are you?" asked Eddie.

"Fine," said Peter.

"How is everybody at your house?" asked Beth.

"Fine," said Peter.

"How are things going at school?" asked Caroline.

"Fine," said Peter.

The girls exchanged knowing looks. "Well, did you come over to see us about something?" asked Beth finally.

Peter nodded.

"About what?" asked Caroline.

"Jake and Josh and Wally really, really, really want those pictures back," said Peter.

"What pictures?" asked Caroline innocently.

"You know. The ones of us acting silly with the Bensons," said Peter.

"Oh. *Those* pictures!" said Eddie. "Well, I don't think we've finished looking at them yet, Peter. Some of them are so silly we just want to look at them a long, long time."

Peter grinned. "Did you see the one of me in a diaper?"

"Yeah, that was silly, all right," said Beth. "But the one of Josh in his Batman underpants was my favorite."

"That's the one Josh really, really, really wants back the most," said Peter.

"Well," said Beth. "We're going to have to think about this, Peter. Of course we'll give them back eventually. They don't belong to us, after all. We just have to figure out what we want to do with them first."

Peter gave a long sigh. He leaned over and rested his

elbow on the lamp table beside the chair, then put his chin in his hand. "Well, I guess I can't go home, then," he said.

"Why not?" asked Eddie.

"Because Josh told me not to come home without the pictures."

The girls tried not to laugh. "Imagine that!" said Eddie.

"I guess you'll just have to live here for a while, then, won't you?" said Caroline. "Of course you'll stay for dinner?"

"What are you having to eat?" asked Peter.

"Chop suey, I think. But I know for sure Mom made a fudge pie."

"Yeah!" said Peter brightly, straightening up again. "I'll stay!"

"Are you girls ready for dinner?" Mrs. Malloy called.

"Yes, and Peter's staying for dinner too, Mom," called Beth.

"Oh? Really? Well, I'll put on another plate, then," said her mother.

When the family gathered in the dining room, Peter took a chair. He didn't seem too sure about the chop suey, taking only a little bit of rice and a small helping of vegetables but his eyes drifted regularly to the kitchen and the chocolate fudge pie sitting on the counter in plain view.

"So what's happening at your house these days, Peter?" asked Coach Malloy. "Everybody doing okay?"

"The answer to whatever you want to know, Dad, is 'fine,' " said Eddie. "I thought I'd save you the trouble of asking."

"I see," said her father. "Well, I imagine your whole family will be going to the game in Clarksburg on Saturday, Peter. Right?"

"Yes, we're all going," said Peter. He frowned. "I may have to ride with you, though."

"Oh? I'm not sure we have room. Our car only holds five," said Mrs. Malloy.

"Uh . . . Mom . . . Peter may be staying over tonight. He can use one of our sleeping bags, can't he?" said Caroline.

"What's this?" asked Coach Malloy. "You're not running away from home, are you, Peter?"

"Just for a little while," Peter told him.

"Doesn't your mother know you're here?" asked Mrs. Malloy.

"Just my brothers," Peter answered.

"Peter Hatford, you go to the phone right now and tell your mother where you are," said Mrs. Malloy. "Tell her it's fine with me if you stay for dinner, but she's got to know where you are. She must be worried."

"O-kay," said Peter reluctantly. He slid off his chair. "But Jake and Josh and Wally aren't going to like it."

Under his breath, Coach Malloy muttered, "Jake and Josh and Wally can go jump in the lake, as far as I'm concerned. We can't have kids appearing and disappearing whenever they get the notion."

"Excuse me," said Caroline. "I just want to make sure he really talks to his mom and not just his brothers."

"Good idea," said Mrs. Malloy.

Caroline went out into the hallway and stood beside Peter as he called home.

"Hi, Wally," said Peter. "Can I talk to Mom?"

Caroline bent down so she could listen.

"Peter, where *are* you?" came Wally's voice. "What's taking so long?"

"I'm eating dinner," said Peter.

There was an anguished wail at the other end of the line. *"Dinner?"*

"I have to talk to Mom!" Peter insisted. "Mrs. Malloy *said*!"

And the next thing Caroline knew, Mrs. Hatford's voice came on the line. "Peter? Is that you? Where *are* you?"

"I'm having dinner at the Malloys' and I'm going to sleep in a sleeping bag," said Peter.

"You most certainly are not!" cried his mother. "Peter, have you lost your mind? You can't just wander over to somebody's house and stay for dinner and sleep in a sleeping bag!"

"I have to," said Peter. "I can't come home."

"Why can't you come home?" Mrs. Hatford demanded.

"Because Jake and Josh and Wally said I couldn't come home without the pictures, and Eddie and Beth and Caroline want to look at them some more, so I'm going to live over here for a while."

"Peter Hatford, you pick up your feet and get yourself home this very minute!" Mrs. Hatford was practically screaming. "This house is a zoo, I tell you! A living, breathing zoo!"

"Okay," said Peter.

"Peter!" his mother continued. "You go back to the table and thank Mrs. Malloy for whatever you ate so far. Then you wipe your mouth on your napkin and carry your dishes to the sink, and you go out the door and come home. Do you understand me?"

"Okay," said Peter. He hung up the phone and walked back into the dining room, Caroline at his heels.

"Thanks for what I ate so far, but I have to go home. Mom said," Peter told them.

"Oh, I'm sorry," said Mrs. Malloy. "Can't you even finish your dinner?"

"Mom said to pick up my feet and come home," Peter told her. He wiped his mouth on his napkin, picked up his plate, and carried it to the kitchen.

"Now, what was *that* all about?" Coach Malloy asked.

"Don't ask, George, don't ask," said Mrs. Malloy.

Caroline went into the kitchen with her own empty plate and got there just in time to see Peter hurriedly stuff something into his pocket. He grinned at her sheepishly and went back through the dining room.

63

"Goodbye," he said.

"Well, it was nice to see you, Peter," said Mrs. Malloy. "We'll invite you to dinner another time."

"Yes, we'll see you at the game Saturday," said the coach. "Tell your dad hello for me."

Peter went out the front door and closed it as Beth took her plate to the kitchen.

"Hey!" she yelled.

"Now what?" asked Mrs. Malloy.

Beth came back into the dining room carrying the chocolate fudge pie. There was a large hole in the middle of it, as though someone, with an insistent thumb, had carved out a bite for himself.

■ ■ ■ ■ ■ ■ ■ ■ ■ ■ ■

Nine

■

Letter to Georgia

Dear Bill (and Danny and Steve and Tony and Doug):

Boy, did you guys ever goof up! You know those pictures we took a year ago? A really stupid picture of each of us, so that if one of us ever betrayed the others, we'd have an embarrassing picture of him to show around school? Well, guess who has them now? Right. Caroline and her sisters.

WHY did you leave them in your basement when you moved? WHY didn't you take them with you?

The Whomper, The Weirdo, and the Crazie have probably been having laughing fits over them. Beth found them on top of a heating duct and the girls won't give them back. Beth says they want to look at them a little longer.

I can't stand it. You know what I'm wearing in my picture? My old bunny pajamas—the ones with feet and floppy ears. They were way too small for me then, and now Peter wears them.

Just remember that you guys have pictures in that album too. Remember how you're dressed up like a ballerina, Steve? With a ribbon in your hair? One false move by us and those pictures will probably make the rounds at school. We tried sending Peter over to sweet-talk the girls into giving them back, but no luck.

The weird thing is, the only people who seem to be getting along right now are Jake and Eddie, probably because they're on the same baseball team. And somehow I have to stay home the day of the championship game because Mom's in charge of the yard sale of the Women's Auxiliary of the Buckman Fire Department, and someone has to guard the stuff that day till she gets back from the game. The sale, of course, happens to be on our driveway, in our front yard, up on our front porch the exact day of the game.

You guys sure did a number on us by moving away, letting the Malloys rent your house, and leaving those pictures in the basement. What do you have to say for yourselves?

Wally (and Jake and Josh and Peter)

P.S. I'd send this by e-mail but stuff for the yard sale is piled in my room blocking my computer. It'll have to go by snail mail, and no telling when you'll get it.

Ten

■

Game Two

On the way to school the next morning, the only two people who were talking to each other were Jake and Eddie. They talked about the Clarksburg team—what they had heard about the pitcher and who was most likely to strike out.

Behind them on the sidewalk, Caroline and Wally glared at each other, and Josh glared at Beth, while Peter strolled along at the rear, humming a little song and running his hand along a row of azalea bushes.

Wally didn't think he could ever be friends with the Malloy girls again. If Caroline ever—*ever*—brought that picture of him in his bunny pajamas to school, with *whiskers* at the sides of his face, even, he would be laughed right out of fourth grade.

He didn't know if he was angrier at the girls for not giving the pictures back or at the Bensons for leaving them behind in the first place. How could they have forgotten *those*? You don't just take the most humiliating pictures of each other you can possibly imagine and then go off and leave them on top of a heating duct in your basement! You especially don't go off and leave them when a family of *girls* is going to rent your home for a year, especially girls like the Malloy sisters, who had caused Wally more trouble in the ten months they had been living there than the Bensons had caused Wally his whole life!

And yet . . . had *he* thought to remind the Bensons to take those pictures with them? Had he even remembered where the pictures were hidden? Had his brothers thought to remind them either?

When he was in his seat, leaning forward so that Caroline couldn't tickle him with her ruler, he tried to concentrate on the next week's assignments, which Miss Applebaum was explaining to the class. But when her back was turned and she began writing the new spelling words on the board, Wally heard a soft voice behind him saying, "Hippity-hop, little bunny, hippity-hop," and he felt his ears beginning to turn red. He didn't know which he disliked more at that moment— Caroline Lenore Malloy or his ears.

At recess, Eddie and Jake went over by the fence to practice pitching and catching. Wally stood glumly off to one side with Josh, but their minds were on other things. Finally Josh spoke:

"There's only one thing left to do: get embarrassing pictures of the girls. Then we'll say that if they don't give those pictures back, we'll put their pictures in that glass case by the auditorium, and by the time the principal sees them, everyone in the whole school will have seen them first."

"Yeah? How are we going to get embarrassing pictures of the girls? Hide in their bathroom? We *posed* for those pictures, remember?" said Wally.

"Yeah, that's the problem," said Josh. "I can't think of a way to do it either."

■

It was the day of the second baseball game, and cars full of excited players and their parents and friends were on their way to Clarksburg. It seemed to Wally that in every other car they passed was someone they knew. Horns honked. People waved to each other, and by the time they got to Clarksburg High School, the bleachers were beginning to fill up. Mr. Hatford, who had taken the day off work from the post office, and Mrs. Hatford, who had taken a day off from the hardware store, gave Jake a final pat on the back and a squeeze of the shoulder.

"Good luck, Jake. Just play your best," his mother said.

"Get out there and show 'em what you've got, son," said his father.

It seemed to Wally that Eddie was in better form than she'd been for the first game. She seemed excited but not too nervous. Buckman was to bat first, and Eddie was first in line. She swung the bat, the ball sailed right over the head of the center fielder, and Eddie made it home. Clarksburg was beginning to look nervous, and the Buckman fans, especially the Malloys, clapped and cheered.

But Clarksburg didn't have anything to be ashamed of, because they had just as good a batter on their team. Wally didn't study the clouds this time. He didn't hang over the edge of the bleachers looking for ants or think about whether the ball diamond might have been a battlefield in the Civil War and whether there were ghosts of soldiers around. He kept his eyes on the ball, and once, when Jake threw a really fast pitch, he caught Caroline Malloy looking down the bleachers at him and smiling, and he started to smile back before he remembered they were enemies. He turned his eyes toward the pitcher's mound again. All Caroline saw when she looked at him, he was sure, was Wally in his two-sizes-too-small bunny pajamas with floppy ears and feet.

Both teams played well, but the game wasn't especially exciting, Wally decided. After the one home run that Eddie made, there weren't any others. Not until the seventh inning did either team score again.

By the final inning, Buckman was ahead by a run. Clarksburg, however, was at bat, and tension was rising.

This time Eddie was pitching and Jake was at shortstop. There were players on first and second. A tall boy stepped up to bat, and the Clarksburg crowd began cheering. All he had to do was hit the ball between two of the outfielders, and his team might get not just one run, not just two, but three. Wally swallowed. So did Josh, beside him.

The boy gripped his bat, his eyes on Eddie. Eddie stood still for a moment, seeming to think it over. Glancing quickly at both runners, she faced the batter again, lifted one foot off the ground, and threw. Strike one. Maybe there was hope yet, Wally thought.

The umpire leaned forward. Eddie pitched again. The batter stood motionless.

"Ball one," the umpire said.

This time Eddie took a longer pause, figuring what to do. Then her arm went back, and before anyone expected it, the ball was on its way. The batter swung, the bat connected, and just as he must have planned it, the tall boy hit a line drive between third base and shortstop.

Jake was in control, however. One arm swooped down and he caught the ball with a soft *plop* in his glove.

"Out!" yelled the umpire. But Jake wasn't through yet.

Both base runners were going at top speed. They skidded around to head back. Jake tagged the boy from second on the shoulder.

"Out!" the umpire yelled again.

Jake wheeled around and fired the ball toward first base. The first baseman caught it and put one foot on the bag before the runner could get back.

"Out!" came the umpire's voice again over the cheers from Buckman fans. All three Clarksburg batters were out.

"A triple play!" Josh yelled.

Out on the field, Eddie was jumping up and down. The second baseman had leaped onto Jake's back, and the rest of the team was swarming around him, throwing their gloves in the air and cheering. The Clarksburg team wasn't cheering, of course, but they too had played well and the score was close.

"Jake, that was something else, let me tell you!" said the coach. "With Eddie's home run and your triple play, I don't think we've ever played better."

Jake beamed. All the Hatfords were out on the field now, slapping him on the back and talking excitedly. It felt pretty good to be a brother of one of the best sixth-grade ballplayers in the school district, Wally thought. Baseball wasn't so bad when he could sit up in the bleachers and watch his brother make a triple play. Maybe if there were triple plays more often, he wouldn't feel like watching the clouds, or the ants carrying crumbs, or a spider weaving a web. If baseball had a little more action, maybe there would be a little more to watch.

The car was full of excited chatter as the Hatfords drove home that evening. Peter thought the town should have a parade in Jake's honor, even though the triple play had happened so fast Peter hadn't even seen it and couldn't describe what it was if he tried.

"Well, at least your team will make it to the third game," said Mr. Hatford. "That much is sure."

"And I'll just bet they'll be one of those two teams playing the championship game," said Mrs. Hatford. "I'm certainly glad that Wally is going to watch over the sale tables on the twenty-ninth, because I wouldn't miss that final game for the world. Not if Jake is playing."

The Women's Auxiliary yard sale! Wally had almost forgotten about it. Now that baseball had suddenly gotten so exciting, he wanted more than ever to be at the championship game instead of sitting with a bunch of lampshades.

Still, that wasn't the worst thing that could ever happen to him. If that was all he had to worry about, it was only a little thing. Then he remembered: the pictures. The bunny pajamas. He had been feeling so good before, about being the brother of Jake Hatford, and now . . .

Wally began to think that for the rest of his life, perhaps, the Malloy girls would take those pictures with them wherever they went, and they would always, always be laughing behind his back.

■ ■ ■ ■ ■ ■ ■ ■ ■ ■ ■

Eleven

■

Act Two

"Well," said Eddie as her family went into the house after the game. "I guess I've got my zip back."

"You have indeed!" said her father. "You played like your old self this afternoon. Between you and Jake, I'd say the coach has himself a pretty good team this year."

Eddie, Jake; Eddie, Jake; Eddie, Jake; Eddie, Jake . . . , thought Caroline in the backseat. As glad as she was for Eddie, as much as she wanted the Buckman Badgers to win the championship, she was sick of hearing about it all the time.

She was tired of Eddie being the center of attention day after day, week after week. Yet, short of running across the baseball field in her underwear, she couldn't think of a single way to focus the attention on herself for a change. Just long enough to remind everyone that she was the girl who would someday—*some*day—have her name in lights on Broadway, and people would say,

"Oh, yes! We knew her when she lived in Buckman, West Virginia."

The only answer was to get right to work finishing act two of her play, so as soon as they got inside, Caroline went up to her room and shut the door. She came down only long enough to have lunch and dinner, and by evening she was ready to knock on Beth's door.

"I finished act two, Beth," she said. "Do you want to hear it?"

Beth was in the middle of her math homework. When Beth did math, she put her notebook and papers on the floor, then stretched across her bed, her head and arms hanging down one side, and wrote on the paper from above. The way to do math, she declared, was to let the blood rush to her head. Only then could she figure it out.

"Okay," Beth said, wriggling her body back up on the bed. "I'm ready for a break." She propped her pillows against the headboard and leaned back, closing her eyes. "Shoot," she said.

Caroline perched on the edge of Beth's bed and held her tablet out in front of her.

Act two, scene one: Still morning in the cottage on the beach. Nancy sits at the table drinking a cup of coffee. The clock on the wall says ten o'clock.

NANCY: I think I must have dreamed it all. Jim has probably gone out for a walk. There isn't any slime here at all. And yet, the telephone still doesn't work. I know he'll be back any minute and then he'll explain the whole thing.

The lights fade out and come on again. The clock on the wall says two o'clock. Nancy is at the table having lunch.

NANCY: Well, if he's gone for a walk, it's a long one. Maybe I should go look for him.

The lights fade out and come on again. The clock on the wall says six o'clock. Nancy is at the table having dinner.

NANCY: Something's happened, I know it! As soon as I eat, I'll go look for him.

Act two, scene two: Daylight is beginning to fade and Nancy is walking along the beach. Suddenly she stops and a look of horror crosses her face.

"Like this, Beth," Caroline said, raising her eyebrows as high as they would go, opening her eyes wide, and shaping her mouth in the form of an O.

NANCY: Here are the same tracks that Jim and I saw in the sand yesterday. They are hardly human, and yet they don't belong to any animal I know. It's as though a creature from outer space was dragging something. Oh, no! Could it have been dragging Jim?

She faints.

Caroline put her tablet down. "Well, how do you like it?" she asked.

"That's it? That's the end of act two?" asked Beth.

Caroline nodded.

"Well, I don't see how a woman whose husband is missing can eat breakfast, lunch, and dinner," said Beth.

"She has to keep up her strength," said Caroline.

"Whatever," said Beth.

"You don't like it!" said Caroline.

"I didn't say I didn't like it. I just can't quite believe it."

"Everything will be made clear in the end," said Caroline. "Everything will come together in act three."

"Good," said Beth. "I can wait."

■

On Sunday afternoon, Caroline tucked the play under her arm and went over to the Hatfords'. She knocked on the door, and when Peter answered, she said, "I'd like to see Wally, please."

"Did you bring the pictures?" asked Peter.

"No," said Caroline. "This is business."

"Okay," said Peter. He opened the door wider and Caroline stepped inside.

Wally came downstairs in his stocking feet. He still had on his Sunday clothes, but his shirttail was hanging out in back.

"What do you want?" asked Wally.

"Come out on the porch, Wally. We're going to talk business," she said. And then, to Peter: "Go back inside, Peter. This is personal."

"Okay," said Peter, and shut the door after them.

"What is it?" asked Wally.

Caroline sat down on the steps. "I have a proposition to make. How much do you want those pictures back?"

"You're going to give them to us?" asked Wally, looking wary.

"I didn't say *give*," said Caroline. "I asked how badly you wanted them back."

"What do you think?" said Wally. "Badly. A lot."

"Okay, here's the deal," said Caroline. "I want something a lot too. You've heard the first act of my play. I want to read the rest to you, and you tell me how you like it. Then . . . *then* . . . you perform it with me in front of the class. If you do that, I'll give you the pictures back."

"No way! I can't!" said Wally. "I'm not an actor."

"Well, just read your part, that's all. You don't have to do anything."

"But I don't even like it!"

"You don't understand it yet, Wally. Once you hear act three, you'll understand it, and if you understand it, you'll probably like it. And even if you don't, well . . . you don't want that picture of you in your bunny pajamas to go around school, do you?"

"No!" said Wally.

"Okay, then. I just want you to sit right here and listen to act two, and then tell me what you think," said Caroline.

"If I listen to the play and read it with you in class—just *read* it—you'll give me the picture of me in my bunny pajamas?" Wally asked.

"Yes," said Caroline.

"And you'll give me the rest of the pictures too?"

"Yes," said Caroline. "But we can't tell *any*body. If Beth and Eddie find out I gave those pictures back, they'll kill me."

"Why? What do they want to do with them?" asked Wally.

Caroline looked deep into Wally's eyes. "Blackmail," she said.

"You mean they'd use them to make us do anything they want?"

"That's right."

"That's exactly what you're doing to me!" said Wally. "You're making me read a play in front of the class."

"Correct," said Caroline.

"That's blackmail!" said Wally.

"Bingo," said Caroline.

■

A half hour later, Caroline took her play home.

"Where have *you* been?" asked Beth.

"I just read act two to Wally Hatford and he listened," said Caroline.

"So?" said Beth. "What else could he do? Did he *like* it?"

"I don't know," said Caroline. "But guess what? He's

going to read Jim's part in front of our class so that I can get an A-plus. If he didn't like it, do you think he'd do *that*?"

"How did you get him to say yes?" asked Eddie from across the room. "Wally Hatford wouldn't do that unless he was hanging upside down over the Grand Canyon by his heels."

"Well, something like that," said Caroline, and went on up to her room to write act three.

Twelve

■

Letter from Georgia

Wally (and Jake and Josh and Peter!):

You've got to be kidding! Did the girls really find those pictures? We are doomed, man! We are dead meat! We are roadkill!

I don't know how we could have forgotten to take them with us. Steve thought Tony had them and Tony thought Steve had them, and the rest of us didn't even know where they were.

You've got to get those pictures back, Wally! I don't care what you have to do to get them, just DO it! If anybody sees that picture of me blowing soap bubbles, with a rip in the seat of my pants, I'll never be able to show my face around Buckman again.

Just GET them, Wally! I'm begging you! Write and tell me you did!

Bill (and Danny and Steve and Tony and Doug)

■ ■ ■ ■ ■ ■ ■ ■ ■ ■ ■

Thirteen

■

More Visitors

When Wally's brothers went to baseball practice on the Monday before the third game, Wally walked home alone. He didn't feel like watching Jake practice. He was afraid that if he was around Jake and Josh for very long, he might let it slip—what he was going to do to get their pictures back. And the reason he didn't want it to slip was because he didn't entirely trust Caroline Malloy to keep her promise.

Not that she would deliberately lie to him, but she might not actually have the pictures. Eddie or Beth might have put them away for safekeeping, and no matter what Caroline told Wally about giving them back, she might not be able to do it. And he would have made a fool of himself in front of the class for nothing. No, if he was to suffer, he would suffer alone.

The second reason he didn't want his brothers to know was . . . well, maybe Wally would have to do a little blackmail of his own. The twins were always getting Wally to do things he didn't want to do. And if he had the pictures, he could say no and mean it. He could say that if they made him do whatever it was he didn't want to do, he would take their pictures to school. He could only do this once, of course, because they would pulverize him if he tried it twice and didn't give the pictures back, but maybe he should hang on to them for an emergency.

He opened the door with his key and went to the kitchen. Now that he was ten years old, he had his own key. His mother didn't call to see if the boys were all right because she thought they were all at the school watching Jake practice. So Wally prepared to enjoy having the house to himself.

First he got down the crackers and peanut butter. He got out the cheese. He found the corn chips and the pickles and the pitcher of cold tea, the applesauce and leftover macaroni. Then he sat down at the table.

It wasn't very often that Wally had the house to himself, and it was nice. It was great, in fact, without Peter's constant chatter and Jake's complaining and Josh's bragging about this or that.

Wally propped his feet up on the chair at the end of the table, smeared a cracker with peanut butter, placed a little square of cheese on top of the peanut butter and a piece of pickle on top of the cheese. He was just about to pop it all into his mouth when the doorbell rang.

Wally put down the cracker and walked to the front

door. When he opened it, he saw two women with purses tucked under their arms. One had on a pink jacket and the other wore her hair in a braid over one shoulder.

"Hello," said the woman in the pink jacket. "Are you one of the Hatford boys?"

"Yes," said Wally.

"We understand that this is where the things for the Women's Auxiliary yard sale are being stored," the woman said.

"Not till the last Saturday of the month," Wally said. "Sorry."

"Oh, but we've heard that some things were donated early," said the woman with the braid. She was wearing sandals and had bright red polish on her toenails.

"Well, some things, but most of the stuff is coming the Friday before the sale," Wally explained.

"We'd just like to come in and look at what you have so far," said the woman with the red toenails.

"Oh, I can't let you do that," said Wally.

"But we'll pay for anything we find now and take it off your hands," said the woman in the pink jacket.

"Well . . ." Wally hesitated. He wondered if she'd buy everything that was piled in his room. He didn't know these women, but then he didn't know a lot of women in Buckman. "I'll have to go call Mom," he said.

"Certainly," said the red toenails.

Wally shut the door, but not quite all the way because he didn't want to seem rude, and went to the phone in the kitchen.

The owner of the hardware store answered. "Your mom's with a customer, Wally," he said. "She'll be with you in just a minute."

Mrs. Hatford must have been selling a customer nails, because Wally could hear the sound of nails being poured into one of the metal scoops on the scales. The hardware store had a metal scoop where you put the object being weighed. Then Mrs. Hatford would take little round weights and put them on the other side of the scales, one by one, until both sides of the scale dangled evenly in the air. There was no digital anything in the hardware store, and that, said the owner, was just the way he liked it.

Finally Mrs. Hatford got on the line. "Wally?" she said.

"Mom, I came home from practice early because I was tired of watching Jake, and there are two women out on the porch who want to look at what we've collected for the yard sale so far."

"Who are they?" his mother asked.

"I don't know."

"Well, it doesn't much matter, because we can't let anyone buy anything until the sale opens on the twenty-ninth. That's the rule. We have to be fair. Otherwise people would be sneaking over all the time and buying the best things before anyone else got a chance. Tell them I'm sorry, but they'll have to wait till the last

85

Saturday in May. Goodness, I had no idea the sale would be so popular!"

Wally went back to the door and put his hand on the knob. "I'm sorry," he said as he opened it. Then he stopped. The porch was empty. At that moment he heard the floor creak in the hallway and when he turned around, he saw the two women poking around in the walk-in closet.

"Oh, forgive us, but we're just so eager to see what you have for sale," said the woman in the pink jacket.

"Mom says I can't let you buy anything before the twenty-ninth," said Wally. "Sorry."

The women looked disappointed. "Well, we won't even try to buy anything, then, but if you could just let us look the things over? Have a peek? Just show us where they are?"

Something told Wally that he didn't much like these women. He knew his mother's rule about strangers in the house. "No," he said, and opened the front door wide. "I guess you'll have to go now."

"Of course," said the woman with the red toenails. "We're just too eager. We do love a good yard sale. Thank you anyway, young man."

"You're welcome," said Wally, and shut the door.

He went to the kitchen again and ate his crackers. Then he called his mother and told her what had happened.

"You mean they walked right into our house while you were on the phone with me?" she gasped. "Why,

Wally, they could have been kidnappers! They could have whisked you away before you knew it!" There was a pause. "Did they take anything?"

Wally began to worry. "I don't know. I don't think so."

"Go look in the dining room and see if the green vase is still on the buffet," said Mrs. Hatford.

Wally went into the dining room and looked. "The vase is still there," he told his mother.

"Did they go upstairs?"

"No."

"Well, look in the living room and see if that little marble dish on the coffee table is still there."

Wally went into the living room.

"It's there," he told his mom.

"What about the little picture hanging beside the coatrack in the hall? Is that still there?"

"Just a minute," said Wally. He checked the wall by the coatrack. "Yes," he told his mother. "That's still there."

"Well, I imagine they were just curious, as they said. We get some frenzied shoppers at these sales, let me tell you! But in the future, don't let anyone in unless it's a member of the auxiliary, Wally, and you know who those women are."

"Okay," said Wally.

■

At school the next day, Miss Applebaum said, "Class, you have just one more week to turn in your book reports. I know that some of you may have been waiting

87

for a certain book at the library that hasn't come in yet, and that baseball season is here and a lot of you have been watching the team practice. But there are eleven of you who have not turned in your reports, and you have only seven more days to finish the project." She turned to Caroline. "Caroline, are you still determined to write a ten-page play, or will you do a book report?"

"I'm working on the play, Miss Applebaum," Caroline said. "But I'll have it done in a week and I'll read it to the class."

"I'm sure we're all looking forward to that," the teacher said, and perhaps she didn't hear the low moans that went around the room. A precocious girl who *knows* she is precocious is not always the most popular girl in school. Especially if that girl is a year younger than everyone else, and especially if she is Caroline Lenore Malloy. From *Ohio,* as Caroline would say, meaning that much closer to New York City and Broadway.

After baseball practice that afternoon, the girls went on ahead and Wally walked behind with his brothers.

"Life would be great right now if only we had those pictures," Jake said. "That's the only thing in the world keeping me from being really happy now that I've made the Buckman Badgers."

"We *have* to get them back," said Josh.

"Maybe we should just go to the sheriff and tell him the Malloys have something that belongs to us," said

Wally. "Maybe Dad, as sheriff's deputy, could go over to the Malloys' in uniform and demand them back."

Josh and Jake stared at him.

"Are you nuts?" asked Jake. "Do you think for one minute he'd do that?"

"If it was important enough, he would," said Wally, beginning to waver.

"And what would you tell him was so important?" asked Jake. "A picture of you in your bunny pajamas? A picture of me with spaghetti hanging out of my nose? Get real."

The day didn't seem quite as sunny, somehow, as it had before.

Perhaps because they were out of sorts, everything seemed to irritate them. Peter had a spring cold, for one thing. His nose was dripping and he snuffled constantly.

When they got home and were getting out the cheese and crackers, Josh said, "Peter, you're disgusting! Wipe your nose, will you?"

Peter started to run his sleeve along under his nose, but Wally yelped, "Not snot on your sleeve! Get a Kleenex or something!"

Peter looked around the kitchen for a box of tissues and, not finding any, dug around in the pocket of his jeans and pulled out a rag. As he wiped his nose with that, he smeared chocolate across his face.

"Yuck!" Jake yelled. "What's that?"

Peter looked at the rag in his hand. "Chocolate," he said.

"Where did you get it?"

"When I was having dinner at the Malloys'," Peter said. And because his brothers were still staring, he added, "I went out in the kitchen and took some of their fudge pie, but then I saw Caroline coming, so I grabbed the dishcloth and wiped my mouth and stuffed it in my pocket so she wouldn't see."

Jake's face was wrinkled in disgust as he studied the rag in Peter's hand. "Now it's got chocolate *and* snot all over it!" he said. "What a weird dishcloth. It looks like it's got elastic, too!"

Josh leaned over. "It's got *words* all over it!" He looked even closer. "The words say *Let's play ball!*"

Wally took the rag from Peter's hands and shook it out. Then he held it up by two fingers. The four boys gasped in unison, for Wally was holding a pair of girls' underpants—old underpants with worn elastic and holes all over.

"Let's play ball!?" croaked Jake. "They could only be Eddie's!"

"You mean you've had Eddie's underpants in your pocket all this time?" Wally asked Peter.

Peter shrugged, not knowing if his brothers were angry or not. In a small voice, he said, "I thought it was a dishcloth. It was just lying up there on the counter."

Suddenly the kitchen erupted in wild shouts.

"We're *saved*!" yelled Jake.

"We'll get our pictures back!" cried Wally.

"We'll wash these up and parade them all around school unless the girls make a trade," said Jake.

"Man oh man oh man, have we got them over a barrel!" said Josh.

"Life is sweeeeeet!" said Jake, waving the underpants over his head like a lasso.

"Let's call over right now and tell them what we've got," said Wally. "I'll bet they bring back those pictures in a hurry."

"Wait a minute," Jake told him. "Not till after the championship game. I don't want to get Eddie mad before a game."

"And maybe we won't even tell them then," said Josh. "Let's just keep these *Let's play ball!* underpants secret until a really good time to tell them comes along. It's our ace in the hole. It's our lucky break. Have you got that, Peter? Not a word!"

■ ■ ■ ■ ■ ■ ■ ■ ■ ■ ■

Fourteen

■

Game Three

The next-to-the-last game was to be played in Weston, and almost everyone was going.

"Of course I want to see Eddie and the Badgers win," Coach Malloy said that morning, tucking a sweater over his arm, "but I've had to get a substitute to work with my next year's players these last three Saturdays. If the Badgers win, though, it will be worth it."

"And if we don't win?" asked Eddie. "Are we zero? Zip? Zed?"

"If you don't win but you played your best, you're still my spunky gal Eddie, and I'll love you just as much," said her dad.

Caroline had long suspected that Eddie was her father's favorite because she shared his love of sports. At the same time, she knew that if she or Beth ever really needed him, he'd be there for them. It was simply a question of where he'd rather be—at a baseball game watching Eddie pitch, in the living room watching Beth read a book, or at a theater watching Caroline perform. *Duh,* thought Caroline. No question at all.

"Well, I'm ready," said Eddie. "Jake and I play well together. It's good we're on the same team."

"Now, *that's* a switch," said her mother.

It wasn't a long ride to Weston, and Caroline didn't have much time to work on her play on the drive there. She had brought her tablet in case the game proved to be slow and boring, but she doubted, from the last two games, that that would be true.

At the high school ball field, the Malloys saw the Hatfords sitting up in the bleachers and went over to sit beside them. Caroline, however, sat as far away from Wally as she could get, because she didn't want Beth to even begin to suspect that she and Wally had made a bargain—that the gold mine of pictures of the Hatford boys was about to be turned over to the Hatfords themselves in exchange for Wally's taking part in her play.

"We've certainly lucked out on the weather for the games, haven't we?" Mrs. Malloy said to Mrs. Hatford as she sat down beside her. "Not a cloud in the sky! After all the rain in April, I'd say we deserve a little sunshine, wouldn't you?"

"We certainly do," said Mrs. Hatford. "The last thing I want on a Saturday in May is to have these four boys moping about the house because it's raining. Baseball gets us all out. Of course, Tom and I have had to take three days from our jobs to get to the games, but we enjoy it."

Out on the field, the players were warming up. The nine members of the Buckman Badgers were throwing the ball to each other in quick succession and then, at the coach's whistle, reversed the order of throw. They did limbering exercises and leg stretches. Finally, when all members of both teams were accounted for, the Buckman Badgers took their positions on the field, Eddie pitching this time, Jake on first base. The game began.

Eddie adjusted her cap with the big *B* on it. She *was* ready. She pitched just the way she pitched back home in practice games, and the first two Weston Wolverines struck out. But the third batter hit the ball to right field. The ball rolled out so far, in fact, that when the runner was halfway between third base and home plate, he stuck his thumbs in the top of his pants and slowed his run to a walk. He simply swaggered back to home plate.

"Well, *he's* feeling good!" murmured Tom Hatford, laughing.

The next batter struck out, so the Badgers came in to bat.

Three Badgers went to the plate before Jake. The first two struck out, the next doubled, and then Jake was up. He swung at the first pitch and missed. On his second swing he hit the ball to center field and started for first base, while the runner on second went to third and started for home. But as his family watched, Jake turned his ankle rounding first base. The center fielder came charging in to throw the ball to home plate. The runner on third was tagged out. Jake, who had sunk to the ground, had managed to stretch out one leg so that he was touching first base. He sat there rubbing his ankle, obviously in pain.

"Oh, no!" said Mrs. Hatford. "Not at the very start of the game!"

Jake got up, though, wincing, and rested his weight on his other foot.

"I think the coach should take him out," Mrs. Hatford said to her husband.

"Jake would have to be tortured before he'd admit anything was wrong," said Josh.

The coach walked over to Jake and stood talking to him for a moment. Jake smiled and flexed his ankle to prove he was fine.

Beth clapped. "He's okay!" she shouted.

Caroline began to wonder about sports. The slightest mistake, it seemed, could cost the game. A ball that was sent flying just two inches above a fielder's glove. A bat that moved only a fourth of an inch too far to the left.

In the theater an actress had several opportunities to correct a mistake. If she forgot her lines momentarily, she could simply pretend to be thinking. If a telephone rang off cue, she could pick it up and pretend to hold an imaginary conversation. If she tripped on her dress and fell, she could pretend it was part of the action and weave it into the plot. Who would know?

The game continued much as it had before, and when the Badgers batted again, Eddie hit the ball so far out that it was hard for a moment to see where it had gone. Around the diamond she went, touching each base, while the people in the bleachers yelled and screamed. The shamefaced Wolverines' fielder found the ball at last and threw it in.

The score seesawed between the Badgers and the Wolverines. The Badgers' right and center fielders collided during the third inning going after a fly ball, and in the fourth the Wolverines argued that Eddie had failed to touch second base while running from first to third. The umpire ruled in Eddie's favor. By the time the game reached the last inning, the score was tied 5 to 5.

The Badgers' first batter struck out. The next batter was out on an infield fly. Jake, batting next, tripled to right field, but Caroline could tell he was in pain. He was limping in spite of himself.

"Tom, that boy should be home with an ice pack on his ankle!" Mrs. Hatford said. "Do you think I should go down and speak to the coach?"

"I think you should sit right where you are and let Jake and the coach work it out," said her husband.

Eddie was up to bat, her last chance to win the game

for the Badgers. When the Wolverines saw Eddie take her place in the batter's box, they all moved back. The shortstop moved back. The center fielder, the right fielder, and the left fielder all moved back. The families and friends in the bleachers all leaned forward, knowing how hard Eddie could hit.

The ball came at her. Eddie tensed, but then held back.

"Ball one," said the umpire.

The next ball came flying toward Eddie, and she let it go by.

"Strike one," said the umpire.

"What's she waiting for?" Caroline heard someone mutter. "She's going to lose her chance if she doesn't take it."

Eddie gave a glance at Jake on third, touched the bill of her cap, and set her eyes again on the pitcher. The three boys in the outfield moved back farther still. The third and first basemen also took two steps back.

The pitcher, without winding up, quickly lifted one foot and threw.

The second the ball left the pitcher's hand, Jake was on his way toward home. As the ball came to the plate, Eddie turned and squared her body to the pitcher's mound. She slid her right hand up the bat and let the barrel just meet the pitch. It connected with only a little pop, not a pow, and rolled a few feet along the ground, down the first-base line.

Pandemonium broke out as the pitcher and the first

baseman scrambled to pick up the ball and tag Eddie, but she raced past them to first base. There was not enough time to make a play at the plate, and Jake, despite his aching ankle, made it home with the winning run. The Buckman Badgers were on their way to the championship game the following Saturday.

Three of the Badgers piled on Jake and almost knocked him down. Everyone crowded around him and Eddie.

"Smart play, Eddie!" said their coach. "Just as we planned. That was the perfect time for a bunt."

"I caught her signal," said Jake. "Everybody thought she'd whack it, but she took them all by surprise!"

"That's what baseball's about—surprises," the coach said. "Good game, guys! Congratulations, everybody!"

■

On the way home, Caroline listened to her sister chattering happily about the game. She was glad that finally Eddie's wish had come true, the dream Eddie'd had since they had moved to Buckman. If Beth had a dream, as far as Caroline could tell, it was simply to have enough good books to read for the rest of her natural life.

It was Caroline's dream that seemed farthest away. It would be years yet before she saw her name in lights on Broadway. It not only took talent to get to be a famous actress, she decided, it took patience. She could only get there one small step at a time, beginning with the play she had written for her class. And in a few more days, she and Wally would read it for Miss Applebaum and the fourth graders. They might even perform it on-stage for the whole school. And if they made it to the big stage in the auditorium, who was to deny that someday Caroline might even make it to a big stage on Broadway?

Fifteen

■

Act Three

When the Hatfords got home from the game and went up onto the front porch, Mrs. Hatford said, "Who left the window open?"

Wally looked where she was pointing. The window to the right of the front door was raised about six inches.

"I suppose any one of us could have opened it, Ellen," said her husband. "It's been a warm May."

"But we haven't opened any of the downstairs windows yet, only the ones in the bedrooms," she declared. "And if I did open it, I certainly would have closed it before we left."

"Well, it wasn't me," said Mr. Hatford.

Mrs. Hatford looked at each boy in turn.

"Not me," said Jake.

"Not me," said Josh.

Wally insisted he had not tried to open it, and Peter didn't even know how.

"Well, it looks to me as though someone might have tried to get in, then," said Mr. Hatford. "Lucky for us that old window only opens a few inches before it sticks."

"You think one of the girls knows we have Eddie's underpants?" Josh whispered jokingly to Wally. "Maybe one of them was over here looking for them."

Wally grinned and shook his head. "All three girls were at the game, remember?"

"Oh, right," said Josh.

"Who would want to rob *us*?" Mrs. Hatford said as they unlocked the door and went inside. "What do we have except a few items of sentimental value?"

"Maybe just kids fooling around," said Mr. Hatford, and after a quick check of the house, to determine that nothing had been taken, nothing was amiss, and no one had been inside, the Hatfords settled down to enjoy the rest of their Saturday with the memory of Jake's winning run.

Wally had already done his homework for the weekend and was looking forward to being able to do whatever he wanted with the rest of his Saturday and Sunday—namely, nothing. He just wanted to be free to do whatever came into his head. For one thing, he liked to go down to the end of the swinging bridge every spring, especially after a gentle rain, and lift up the large rock that rested just off the path.

He liked to see if the same kinds of bugs stayed there year after year. He always counted the different ones he found. It was a little like a bug hotel. Maybe bugs, too, liked to get away for the weekend.

He was squatting down next to the bare patch he'd uncovered and was trying to poke up the bugs that were scurrying around in all directions when he heard the hollow sound of footsteps on the swinging bridge. Looking up, he saw Caroline coming toward him with her tablet under her arm.

"Goodbye weekend," Wally murmured to himself. No one on earth could ruin a good weekend faster than Caroline Malloy. He didn't have to be in her old play, though. Sure, she was trying to blackmail him with those pictures. Well, he could blackmail her with Eddie's underpants. Should he do it?

"Finished!" she called. "My play is done, and all I have to do is type it up. Want to hear it, Wally?" And without waiting for an answer, she said, "Of course you do. Let's go up on your porch."

Wait, Jake had said. *Let's save the underpants for a time we really need to bargain.*

Well, if this wasn't the time, Wally didn't know what was. He prodded a bit more with his stick. "Can't you read it right here?"

"All right, Wally," she said, "provided you pay attention. Act three, scene one: Evening in the cottage by the beach. Nancy is fixing dinner."

"Doesn't she ever do anything but eat and faint?" asked Wally.

"She's just doing her ordinary everyday routine to calm her nerves," Caroline explained, and continued: "Nancy puts two plates and glasses on the table, then suddenly covers her face with her hands and cries when she realizes Jim is no more."

"How does she know he's no more?" asked Wally. "He disappears the day before and suddenly he's no more, and she goes on eating dinner?"

"Wally, if you keep interrupting you'll never find out," Caroline said indignantly. "Sometimes you have to wait till things reveal themselves. Please save your criticisms until I've finished."

"Okay, but at the end of the second act, she'd fainted, you know. And now she's making dinner. . . ."

"Well, sometimes you have to just guess what went on in between, Wally. A playwright doesn't have to show every little thing. Obviously she woke up or somebody came along and revived her. The audience has to figure some things out for itself."

"Okay," said Wally.

Nancy sits down on a chair and turns to look out the open window facing the sea. There is a faint sound of sloshing and sliding offstage. As Nancy stares mournfully out at the waves, her back to the doorway, the sloshing sound grows louder and louder. Nancy covers her face

*with her hands and sobs. The sloshing and sliding grows
louder still.*

*A shadow appears in the doorway behind her and spreads
across the floor, and the audience sees a kind of shapeless
form coming in sideways, like a mass of primordial green
slime, a sort of giant amoeba, and it slithers and slides
closer, closer, closer, until Nancy hugs herself, as though
she feels a sudden chill. She turns around and screams as
the moonlight coming in the window shines on the giant
amoeba, and the audience sees that it has the face of Jim.
Curtain falls.*

Wally put down his stick and sat back on his heels.
"Is that the *end*?"

"No. Just scene one."

*Scene two: Nancy has fainted again. The giant amoeba
picks her up in his arms and puts her on the couch.
Nancy wakes up and screams again.*

NANCY: Jim! What's happened to you?

JIM: Nothing's happened, my darling. I've been an
amoeba all along but you didn't know. I was sent from
my kingdom down under the sea in disguise to choose
a bride. Now you belong to me.

NANCY: No! No! A thousand times no! Never to
breathe in sweet air again? Never to see the sun rise?
Jim, how could you do this to me? I thought you
loved me.

JIM: I have a greater love for the netherworld. Come
with me and you shall be queen of the waves and caves

of the deep. You shall rule over all the sea creatures of night and dark and ocean depths.

NANCY: No, no, no! I shall die if I leave my earthly home.

JIM: You shall die if you don't.

NANCY: Help! Help! Will no one come and save me?

The door opens and a fisherman comes in, an ice bucket in one hand, a fishing rod in the other.

FISHERMAN: What's the matter? Say, what's this? A giant amoeba?

NANCY: Help! He wants to take me down under the water and make me Queen of the Deep.

The fisherman lifts his ice bucket and hits the amoeba over the head, but he is only sucked into the amoeba and finds himself covered with green slime.

FISHERMAN: No! He's got me!

NANCY: There is no hope.

JIM: There is only night and dark and waves and caves, and you, my darling, Queen of the Deep.

The blob oozes back out of the room, dragging Nancy and the fisherman with him, and all that is left onstage is the fisherman's ice bucket and rod, Nancy's shoes, and Jim's tie.

The End

Wally didn't say a word. He was still thinking about the story.

"Well?" said Caroline, clutching her tablet, her eyes dancing with excitement and anticipation.

"If Jim was an amoeba all along, why did he yell when he left the bedroom that first time? And who was making the sloshing sound when he was with Nancy?"

Caroline didn't seem too sure. "Well, he'd sort of brought the netherworld with him. And the yell was just to trick his wife," said Caroline.

"It's a horrible, sickening play with a bad ending," said Wally.

"But you have to admit there's suspense! People like suspense!" said Caroline.

"Are you sure I get extra credit for being in this play?" asked Wally.

"Yes," said Caroline. "I checked."

"And if I read this play with you, I get to be the amoeba?" Wally asked.

"Yes," said Caroline.

"Then I like it," said Wally. Suddenly things began to look very bright indeed. Maybe Wally did want to be in the play after all. Where else could he cover himself with green slime and drag Caroline Malloy around?

"Really? That's wonderful! I knew you would!" said Caroline. "Who can we get to play the fisherman?"

"What about Peter?" Wally suggested, knowing the twins would never do it.

"Perfect. He'll do it, he's such a sweetie!" said Caroline. "All we need are a few props—a tie, some shoes, an ice bucket, a fishing rod, some golf clubs, dishes . . ."

"What do we do for the green slime?"

"We've got some left from Halloween," said Caroline. "I'll tell Miss Applebaum that we'll perform my play on Friday, okay?"

"Okay," said Wally. Oh, yeah! He was going to like playing an amoeba just fine.

He went into the house, where Peter was working a puzzle on the floor in the living room.

"Hey, Peter," Wally said. "You want to be in a play?"

"What play?"

"A play Caroline's written. We have to put it on in front of our class."

"What do I have to do?"

"Hit me over the head with an ice bucket and let me cover you with green slime."

"Cool!" said Peter.

■ ■ ■ ■ ■ ■ ■ ■ ■ ■ ■

Sixteen

■

Getting Ready

Thursday after dinner, Caroline went to the Hatfords' carrying some props for the play. She handed one of her father's old ties to Wally.

"You'll want to wear this, because it's the only thing left of Jim after he turns into the giant amoeba," she said.

She handed a fishing rod and a Styrofoam ice bucket to Peter. "When you swing at Wally, you only *pretend* to hit him," she said.

She held out an old pair of her mother's high-heeled shoes. "And these will be all that's left of me after the amoeba carries me off," she said.

They went through a brief rehearsal in the Hatfords' living room, and would have run through it again—all but the green slime, which they were saving for the real performance—if Mrs. Hatford hadn't called down from upstairs.

"Wally? The twins went shopping with your father, and I could use some help up here."

Wally went upstairs, Caroline behind him.

Mrs. Hatford was seated on a folding chair in the middle of Wally's bedroom, surrounded by bags and boxes and baskets.

"Everything that people bring tomorrow night for Saturday's sale will go downstairs," she explained. "The auxiliary women are coming over then to check it all in and put price tags on it. But meanwhile, there's all this stuff people donated in advance. I have to list everything we've stored in your room. Maybe Caroline could help too while she's up here."

"Sure," said Caroline. "What should I do?"

"As each of you picks up an item and tells me who it's from, I'll write it down on this clipboard. The women will price them tomorrow. After we've listed something, set it over there by the door."

Caroline sat down on the floor beside a bushel basket, and Wally chose a box crammed between his computer and a couple of paper bags.

"This basket is from Susan Kemp," said Caroline. "One sugar bowl . . . one cream pitcher . . . two candy dishes . . ."

"Wait a minute, don't go too fast," said Mrs. Hatford, writing on her clipboard. "Susan's grandfather started the Kemp Real Estate business, you know. She's been such a help to the auxiliary. . . ."

"One silver serving spoon," Caroline continued. "Four sets of salt and pepper shakers . . ."

When the basket of dishes had been cataloged, Mrs. Hatford turned to Wally. He dug down in the box beside him and took out an old photograph with a thick backing and frame. "A picture of somebody's grandparents, I guess," he said.

"Who donated it, Wally?"

Wally checked the box. "Jenny Bloomer."

Mrs. Hatford wrote it down. "Oh, yes. Jenny. She's descended, you know, from Amelia Bloomer, the famous suffragette of the eighteen hundreds."

"What's a suffragette?" asked Caroline. "Like a martyr? Somebody who suffers?"

"No, it's someone who stood up for a woman's right to vote and hold office and do the things women weren't allowed to do back then."

"Oh," said Wally. "One pen and pencil set . . . one leather dictionary . . ."

On it went. Everything in the bags and boxes and baskets in Wally's room had to be taken out and listed, until finally Wally's room looked positively naked and it was the hall beyond his door that was crowded.

"Can you imagine what our house is going to look like tomorrow night when all the women bring their things over?" asked Mrs. Hatford. "We'll hardly be able to walk through the rooms!" She looked at Wally. "Don't worry," she said. "As soon as the game is over Saturday, the women will all come back here to take over, and you can leave. We'll have everything in place before we go, and all you and Mrs. Larson will have to do is guard the tables and not let anyone buy anything before we get back."

"What if it rains?" asked Wally.

"It's not supposed to rain. If it does, we have large sheets of plastic you can use to cover the tables."

"What if there's a big crowd and I can't watch everybody at once?"

"There won't be. Most of Buckman will be at the game. The championship game's being played here, you know, right at your school."

"I'll be here to help too, Wally," said Caroline. "I'd be too nervous to watch Eddie play the last game. Just hearing them cheer will be enough excitement for me."

"Really? You'll be here? Hey, Mom. What about if we leave Caroline in charge and I go to the game?" Wally asked.

"We'll do no such thing," said his mother. "I need someone besides Mrs. Larson to keep an eye on the tables. People can look, but they can't buy, and three sets of eyes watching over the place are better than two."

"It'll be sort of fun, Wally," said Caroline. "We'll be like security guards at the mall."

When they had checked the last of the bags out of Wally's room, they found more boxes in his closet. There were even some under his bed.

"One toy tea set . . . ," began Caroline. "One child's dress, size four . . . one blue umbrella . . ."

III

"Who's the donor?" asked Mrs. Hatford.

"Catherine Collier," said Caroline.

"Catherine's great-great-grandfather opened the second bank here in Buckman," said Mrs. Hatford. "She herself helped found the Women's Auxiliary. We couldn't do half the things we do if it weren't for Catherine Collier." It seemed to Caroline as though every woman in Buckman had a history behind her.

Wally's room began to look so empty that Caroline began to wonder if they were carting half his own belongings downstairs with the rest. But Wally sure looked happy about having his room to himself again.

"Mom," he said. "Promise me you won't ever take on the job of running the Treats and Treasures yard sale again. Not at our house."

"If I ever do," said his mother, "it will not be for a long, long time, and you'll be off at college by then, I imagine."

■

"Okay," Caroline said at the front door. "I'll bring all the props to school tomorrow: golf clubs, ice bucket, fishing rod, green slime, tie, shoes, dishes, and special effects."

"I think a book report would be easier," said Wally.

"Of course it would be easier, Wally, but would it be better? No! Did you know that great actresses have plays written especially for them? When you're really famous, movies are made for you alone. People beg you to be in their plays or their movies. If I could write my own plays *and* star in them, I'd be a huge success."

"Don't forget the pictures," said Wally. "You know what you promised."

"Oh. Right!" said Caroline. "The pictures." Did she only imagine it, she wondered, or was Wally trying not to smile?

She started down the walk to the road and the swinging bridge beyond, and then she turned around suddenly to look at Wally again, up on the porch. He *was* smiling, but not at her. He was smiling to himself. He did not look like a boy who had to do something he hated. He looked like a boy who had a secret, and Caroline had a strange feeling that the secret had to do with her and her sisters.

■ ■ ■ ■ ■ ■ ■ ■ ■ ■ ■

Seventeen

■

"A Night to Forget"

When it came time for Caroline to read her play to the class, she got permission to borrow Peter from his second-grade classroom and led him back to Miss Applebaum's room. Peter smiled shyly at the fourth graders, obviously feeling very important to be there.

Wally did not feel as embarrassed as he had thought he would. In fact, knowing how the play would end, he couldn't wait to get started. For too long the Malloy sisters had seemed to get the upper hand in their arguments with the Hatford brothers, but this time, unknown to the girls, it was the boys who were in control.

So when Caroline stood up and announced that she was going to read an original play, "A Night to Forget," Wally stood behind a file cabinet off to one side with Peter and did not come out until Caroline read, "Act one, scene one: A cottage on the beach in a faraway town. Ten o'clock at night. A couple on their honeymoon."

The kids burst into laughter.

"Ha, Wally!" one boy yelled.

"Your *honey*moon!" crooned another.

Wally ignored them.

"Class, let's be quiet now and listen," said Miss Applebaum, and the dialogue began. But as soon as Wally said, "Wasn't that a nice walk on the beach . . . honey?" the class giggled again.

Peter, however, had been assigned to make the sound effects, and as soon as the class heard the sloshing and sliding, which was the noise a balloon half filled with water made as Peter dragged it around the floor behind the file cabinet, the class gave the play its full attention.

"Act one, scene two," read Caroline. "Twelve o'clock at night, Jim and Nancy's bedroom." Then she and Wally had their conversation, and when Wally went offstage with a golf club to investigate the noise (Peter again, with his balloon), and a horrible scream came from behind the file cabinet, some of the girls even jumped.

By the time Wally reappeared as the amoeba, his clothes, his arms, his ears, his hair—everything but his face—were covered in green slime, and the class gave a loud *ohhhhh*. When it was her turn to scream, Caroline did it dramatically and fell to the floor in a faint so convincing that the principal, who was going by, stopped and looked in the door.

Peter tried to miss Wally and just make it look as though he had hit him with the ice bucket, but actually managed to bonk his head. Immediately, of course, he was swept up into the creature's slimy arms. And then the monster from the netherworld, dragging Peter in one hand and Caroline by her ponytail in the other, intoned, "There is only night and dark and waves and caves, and you, my darling, Queen of the Deep."

"Ouch!" said Caroline softly.

Wally looked and sounded so evil at that point, and seemed to be having such a good time dragging Caroline, bumping and thumping, across the floor, that everyone clapped and cheered him on, and when it was over, everyone wanted to feel the green slime for themselves. Wally grinned. He would never have believed he could enjoy performing as much as this.

Miss Applebaum clapped too. "Well," she said. "That was quite a story, Caroline. Thank you, Peter, for taking part. You may go back to your room now, though I think you'll want to wash up first. Wally, I do hope you brought a change of clothes."

He had indeed. When he and Caroline went out into the hall to head for the rest rooms, she said, "You didn't have to be so rough, Wally! But weren't we great? Did you hear how everyone clapped?"

"They really liked the green slime," said Wally, grinning a little.

"*I'd* like to think they liked the whole play! It had

everything—romance, suspense, mystery, terror, science fiction . . ."

"Whatever," said Wally, and went into the boys' rest room to clean up. He didn't even mention getting the pictures back now that he had kept his part of the bargain. He was having too much fun.

■

When Wally and his brothers got home from baseball practice that afternoon, they hardly recognized their house. There were women going in and out the front door. A woman sat at a card table just inside the door writing down each item as it arrived.

The living room looked like an antique store. There were lampshades and trunks and lawn chairs and books; there were coats and platters and galoshes and figurines. An accordion perched on the back of Mr. Hatford's favorite armchair; the couch was covered with dishes. The dining room table was stacked high with clothes to be sorted, and one end of the room was heaped with children's toys.

Mr. Hatford went out to buy Kentucky Fried Chicken for dinner, which he and the boys ate upstairs in Wally's near-empty bedroom, and afterward Peter went out into the hall and stared forlornly down at the women who were still coming and going.

"I liked us better before," he said.

Mr. Hatford laughed. "So did I, Peter, but after to-morrow, it will all be over. All the stuff is going to be moved outside, and we won't have to look at it any longer."

"Why do people buy so much if they just give it away?" asked Peter, coming back into the bedroom.

"A very good question, Peter. Very good. We'll have to ask your mother sometime. But right now we're all focused on tomorrow. Jake plays the championship game and your mom runs the sale. How are you feeling, Jake? Did you have a final practice after school today?"

"Yep. We're playing the toughest team, though—the Grafton Grangers."

"Well, *they're* playing the toughest team too, so don't let that discourage you."

"Hey, hey!" said Jake. "I'm ready."

■

When all the women had gone at last, Mrs. Hatford came upstairs and fell across her bed.

"Think you'll make it?" Mr. Hatford asked as he sat down beside her and rubbed her back, the boys gathering in the doorway.

"I've never been so tired in my whole life," she said. "Even my fingernails ache."

"Who's setting up tomorrow?" Wally asked.

"The men. All the husbands are going to come over at seven, set up the tables on the porch and lawn and driveway, and put out all the stuff. We've color-coded every item, so that the things that sell for between one and five dollars will go on one table, things going for five to ten dollars will be on another, and . . . so . . . on. . . ." Her voice dropped off as she sank into sleep. Mr. Hatford put one finger to his lips and sent the boys back to their rooms.

■

After Wally went to bed that night, he realized he had forgotten to demand those pictures back from Caroline now that the play was over. Well, when she came the next day to help with the sale, she'd just better have them with her, or perhaps *that* was when he'd tell her about Eddie's LET'S PLAY BALL! underpants that they were going to run up the flagpole if they didn't get their album back.

He turned on his side and smoothed out his pillow. With his ear off the pillow momentarily, however, he thought he heard a noise. Footsteps. He had thought that the rest of the family was in bed, but then the sound came again. It almost sounded as though it was coming from the front porch.

Wally sat up and listened. Then he got up and went to the door of his bedroom. All the other bedroom doors were closed, and there was no light shining from under any of them.

Wally felt his way along the dark hall and slowly descended the stairs, being careful to avoid the next to the last step because it squeaked. If there was a robber in the house, Wally didn't want to be heard.

At the bottom of the stairs, he looked all about him—the living room, the dining room . . . There was certainly no one there that he could see. Wally went over to the front door. For a minute he thought of turning on the light to see if anyone was out there. Then he saw a circle of light—the beam of a flashlight—moving across the grass in the front yard and disappearing at last in the trees.

Eighteen

■

Mystery

It seemed as though everyone in Upshur County was at the Buckman Elementary school baseball field on Saturday. Shortly after the Malloys were seated on the bleachers and the game with the Grafton Grangers began, Caroline whispered in her mother's ear, "I'm going over to the Hatfords' and help Wally with the sale."

"You're not going to watch the rest of the game?" Mrs. Malloy asked in surprise.

"I can't!" Caroline wailed softly. "I've got butterflies in my stomach. But I don't want Eddie to know I've left, so I'm just going to slide through the bleachers. You'll have to tell me about it afterwards."

Her mother understood. "All right," she said. "I don't want you fainting dramatically if Eddie misses a ball. I'm sure Wally can use you." She helped Caroline slip down to the ground below. Beth and Coach Malloy didn't even notice that she had gone.

It was very warm for a day in May, and instead of her usual jeans and T-shirt, Caroline had put on a sundress that morning. If she was going to be a security guard at the Hatfords', people were going to see her. And if people were going to be noticing her, she wanted to look her best. She hurried down the sidewalk toward the Hatfords' house but hardly recognized it when she got there.

It looked like a junkyard. An organized junkyard. Every square inch of ground, it seemed, had a table on it with a sign listing prices for those items. There were aprons and axes, teddy bears and ties. A hand-lettered sign at the bottom of the driveway said SALE BEGINS AT NOON.

Already, however, there were a few browsers wandering among the tables, fingering the embroidered bedspreads, checking the price on a cake pan, measuring the width of a plant stand, or trying on a raincoat. Mrs. Larson hovered over the cash box and tried to keep an eye on everyone at once.

"Hi," said Wally, and followed that up with, "Where are the pictures?"

"I couldn't bring them now, Wally, because I came from the game. I didn't think you'd want me taking them *there*," said Caroline.

"If you don't give them to me, Caroline . . . ," Wally said threateningly.

"I *will*! I *promise*!" Caroline said.

Mrs. Larson called them over and handed Wally a Polaroid camera. "I want you to take a picture of every table before we start the sale," she said, half shouting because she could hardly hear herself. "We want to put them in our auxiliary newsletter so the women can see what wonderful donations we had this year. The people of Buckman have never been more generous."

Caroline and Wally wandered up and down the rows of folding tables, checking to see that all was well and pausing while Wally took pictures of table after table. As the photos came out of the camera and began to develop, it appeared that Caroline had somehow managed to be in each one, looking directly into the camera and smiling.

The sugar bowl and creamer from Susan Kemp, the framed photograph from Jenny Bloomer, the copper lamp from Edna Ballinger, the ceramic figurines from the Wheelers . . . a place for everything, and everything in its place. All the while Mrs. Larson, whose voice carried all over the yard, chattered away with neighbors who had come by to check out the sale.

A woman in a blue jacket came up to a display and smiled at Caroline. She smiled at Wally. Then she began walking around the tables, not stopping to look at much of anything until she saw the framed photograph from Jenny Bloomer, showing two stern-looking elderly people in rocking chairs. She picked it up and examined the back.

Over she came to Wally and took a twenty-dollar bill from her purse. "I'll take this, please," she said. "The price says fifteen dollars."

"The sale doesn't start till noon," Wally said. "We're just letting people look."

"But I can't come back at noon," the woman said. She put the twenty-dollar bill on the table where the framed photograph had been.

"I can't sell it now. I can't give you change," Wally said, reaching for the photograph. "It's against the rules." He looked over at Mrs. Larson, hoping she would come and talk to the woman. But Mrs. Larson had her back to them and was chatting with someone else. When Wally turned toward the woman in the blue jacket again, she was walking down the driveway, the framed photo in her arms, the twenty-dollar bill left behind.

Caroline saw, and shrugged. "What can we do, Wally? She wanted it, she got it. She paid for it, after all, and the auxiliary gets to keep the change."

"I suppose so," said Wally. He picked up the twenty-dollar bill and walked beside Caroline to Mrs. Larson. They waited politely while Mrs. Larson said goodbye to the woman she'd been talking with and that woman. turned to go.

Caroline nudged Wally. "Get a look at those bright red toenails," she giggled.

Wally turned and stared at the woman who had been talking with Mrs. Larson. Then he turned some more and saw her catch up farther down the sidewalk with the woman who had taken the framed photo.

Suddenly Wally grabbed Caroline's arm. "Caroline!" he gasped. "It's them!"

"Who?" asked Caroline.

"The women who tried to get in our house. The last time I saw them, the one with the photograph was wearing a pink jacket. And I'd recognize the red toenails on the other one anywhere."

"They must want that framed picture really bad," said Caroline.

"Yeah, but why? They must know something about it that Jenny Bloomer didn't know. Follow them!" Wally said.

"*What?*" said Caroline.

"You've got to follow them and see where they go! We might have to get that picture back."

"Are you serious?" Caroline asked. She had come over to be a security guard and now she was a detective?

"*Go!*" Wally said. "I can't leave here till Mom gets back."

"I'm going!" said Caroline. "What am I supposed to do if I catch up with them? Bring the picture back?"

Wally wasn't sure. His mother had said no one was to buy anything before the sale opened. "I guess so," he said. "At least find out where they live."

Caroline took off. This, she decided, was a lot more exciting than watching a baseball game. Even a championship game. Far off on the school ball field, she could hear the crowd cheer, then cheer again. Did that mean a hit for the Badgers? Or was it the fans for the Grafton Grangers who were doing the cheering?

No matter, she told herself. *Keep your eyes on that blue jacket, but don't let them know you're following them.* If she was ever given the part of a girl detective, she'd know what it felt like. They turned, Caroline turned. They went up an alley, Caroline went up an alley. At last they went around a corner and up the steps of Mrs. Ritter's Bed and Breakfast. As soon as they were inside, Caroline, too, bounded up the front steps.

Flattening herself against the wall just outside the screen door, she heard a woman's voice call from far inside the house, "Did you have a nice walk, ladies?"

"It was lovely, Mrs. Ritter," one of the women answered, and when Caroline peered around the corner, she saw them going up the big oak staircase to the second floor.

Her heart was thumping hard inside her chest. She softly opened the screen door and slipped inside. She heard an electric mixer back in the kitchen, and she smelled cinnamon as something baked in the oven.

Caroline crossed the oriental rug in the hallway and made her way upstairs, keeping her feet close to the wall, where the steps were less likely to creak.

Even before she reached the top, she could hear the women's excited voices from one of the guest rooms.

"We're in luck, Dorothy. If we'd waited for the sale

to begin, who knows who could have walked off with this!" said one.

"By the time Jenny finds out—"

"Why does she have to know? We're the ones who found the letter in Mother's things. What our cousin doesn't know won't hurt her. That's what she gets for giving away family pictures."

"Hurry up, Marva," the other woman said. "What did the letter say? Just that something of great value was hidden behind the backing?"

"Yes, and we're about to find out what it is," said the first woman. "See how it bulges out back here? You can feel that something's in there, but you probably wouldn't know just by looking. The letter said it was an heirloom the family would want to keep forever."

"Do you need a nail file or scissors or something?"

"No, I can slide the paper open with my finger and work it off the frame. Something's in here, all right."

Okay, Caroline told herself, peeping carefully around the door frame. *Be ready. Whatever's in the back of the picture frame, I've got to grab it and take it to Wally.*

"I'm so nervous!" said the woman in the blue jacket, and then there was the sound of glue pulling away from the wooden frame, and a thick white packet fell out.

Now! Caroline thought.

Like a racehorse from the starting gate, she tore into the room. The women gave startled cries, turning to stare wildly at her. Caroline snatched up the white packet, and with a "Sorry, not for sale," she went streaking out again and down the stairs.

The women shrieked. There was the sound of footsteps coming down the hall after her, then down the stairs. Caroline didn't stop.

"Catch her!" screamed one of the women, but Caroline was out the door and down the steps, the two women thundering along behind.

Down the street she ran, around a corner, through an alley. On the women came. She had to hide. She could probably outrun them if she really tried, but she was getting out of breath. She turned a corner and saw a gas station up ahead. Making a sharp turn beyond the station, she ran along one side into the rest room and locked the door behind her.

Breathing hard, Caroline listened for the women's footsteps, and it wasn't long before she heard them coming. They came around the corner, then slowed, and finally stopped not far from the rest room door.

"Where did she *go*?" one woman cried.

"Who *was* she?" asked the other, panting. "Never on this earth have I—"

"The little thief!"

"She must have known all along what we were after."

"How could she? *We* don't even know what was in there!"

Caroline leaned against the wall in the rest room, her heart thumping painfully. Then slowly, silently, she looked at the white packet in her hands. It appeared to be thin cloth, old cotton, perhaps, and gently she began to unfold it. Layer after layer began to fall away until finally, there in her hands, Caroline found a pair of old-fashioned underpants that reached from the waist all the way down to the ankles, with elastic at the top and bottoms.

Caroline stared. Jenny Bloomer had contributed a picture frame with a pair of women's underpants hidden in the back? Was this a joke or what?

She didn't know. All she knew was that the two women had wanted what was in that picture frame very badly. So whoever these underpants belonged to, they must be very valuable, and it was Caroline's job to see that they were returned to their rightful owner. If she went outside and the women were still there, they would snatch them away from her, she was sure.

Suddenly Caroline knew what to do. She thrust her left foot into the left leg of the underpants. Then she thrust her right foot into the right leg. She pulled the garment up under her sundress and tugged at the elastic around the ankles until the material had bunched up to her knees. Then, the strange underpants swishing against her legs, she opened the door a crack and peered out. The women were walking back toward Mrs. Ritter's Bed and Breakfast, talking and gesturing wildly.

Slowly Caroline emerged. Slowly, stiffly, she walked back along College Avenue to the Hatfords' house as more cheering came from the baseball field. Her hair was wet with sweat, her face flushed. One strap of her sundress had slipped down off her shoulder, and one shoe was untied.

Wally saw her coming. He and Mrs. Larson took a few steps forward.

"Gracious! What excitement!" Mrs. Larson exclaimed. "Those two women had no right coming in here and taking that picture! Jenny Bloomer wanted us to have it for our sale, and everyone should have an equal chance to buy it."

"Did you find out why they wanted it? Did you get what they were after?" asked Wally.

Caroline nodded, and while Wally and Mrs. Larson stared, she simply hiked up her sundress to show the long cotton underpants bunched around her knees.

Nineteen

■

Amelia B.

Wally saw his opportunity. He raised the Polaroid camera and took a picture. Then he started to laugh.

Caroline's face reddened even more as she dropped her dress.

"That?" Wally guffawed as Mrs. Larson kept staring. "*That's* what was hidden in the picture frame? Somebody's old-fashioned underpants?"

"Let me see those!" said Mrs. Larson, going over. She reached down and felt the material that was sticking out below Caroline's sundress. "That is old muslin if I ever saw it. Why, I haven't seen cotton like that since I don't know when. It looks like something out of my grandmother's trunk."

Seeing that they might be valuable, Caroline stepped out of the underpants carefully and held them out for closer inspection.

"What have we here?" Mrs. Larson cried, pointing

to a hand-stitched label on the inside. "Oh, my stars! Look what it says! Amelia Bloomer! Caroline, you have just stepped out of the bloomers of the famous suffragette herself, Amelia Bloomer! Why, these belong in a museum!"

"Those are called bloomers?" Wally asked, putting two and two together.

"Indeed they are!" said Mrs. Larson. "These were Amelia's trademark, you might say. She wore loose trousers like this everywhere she went, sticking out of the bottom of her dress, and they were called bloomers after her. Our very own Jenny Bloomer is related, you know."

"Why would Amelia Bloomer want to wear things like that?" asked Caroline.

"Because she felt that women should be able to do much more than they were allowed to do back then. She wanted them to be able to vote, to hold any jobs they liked, and to wear clothes that let them be more active. She designed her clothes herself."

Another cheer went up from the baseball field, and at that very moment a car drove up and Jenny Bloomer got out.

"I knew I ought to get back before people started arriving, but I hated to leave. The score was tied," she said. "Anyway, I'm here, so what can I do to help?"

"You can explain these," said Mrs. Larson with a smile, and held out the folded bloomers.

"What's this?" asked Jenny.

"These were sealed in the back of the framed photograph you gave to the sale. And look on the inside."

When Jenny Bloomer saw the embroidered name of her distant relative, she gasped. "I knew we were related, but I had no idea I had her bloomers! I didn't even know who those people in the photograph were, we've had it so long. We're moving to a smaller house and I just wanted to sort through some things."

"Well, they certainly made for an exciting morning for us!" said Mrs. Larson loudly. "Tell her, Wally."

"Two women came to the sale early—the same women who wanted to look at our sale stuff before," said Wally. "One of them wanted the picture you donated, but I wouldn't sell it to them, so she just put a twenty-dollar bill down and made off with the picture."

"And I followed them to Mrs. Ritter's Bed and Breakfast and snatched the bloomers away as soon as they fell out the back of the frame," said Caroline.

Jenny Bloomer stared at Caroline. "Was one of those women dark-haired and the other blond?"

"Yes," said Wally and Caroline together.

"Was one of those women short and the other tall?"

"Yes," said Wally and Caroline together.

"And one wore red, red polish on her toenails," offered Caroline.

"Those are my cousins, Dorothy and Marva!" cried Jenny. "Ever since Mother died, they have been pestering me to find out if she left them anything in her will.

That just seemed so greedy to me, because they didn't visit her or write to her when she was sick. So I didn't offer them any of the things I was giving away, just some boxes of letters between their mother and mine. I'll bet one of those letters mentioned something valuable hidden in one of my pictures."

"They did say something about a letter," said Caroline.

"Oh, I know I should have read that correspondence before I gave it away, but I had so many things to sort. I felt I had to give my cousins at least something, though. They probably thought there was money hidden in that picture frame. It wouldn't surprise me if they had used Amelia's bloomers for a dust cloth."

Another cheer came from the direction of the ball field, and a few seconds later, still another. And then one terrific roar, followed by clapping. A few horns began to blow.

"Well, it must be over," said Wally. "I wonder who won."

A few minutes later Peter came running up the sidewalk, followed by the rest of the Hatfords, and everyone was smiling.

"We won!" Peter cried delightedly. "The Buckman Badgers did it!"

The Malloys came up the sidewalk after them.

"Eddie's last hit brought in the winning run!" Beth called.

"And Jake struck out the last batter on Grafton's team!" said Eddie.

"It was a close game," said Coach Malloy, "but I must say, this was one of the best ball games by any sixth graders that I've ever seen."

"Same here," said Mr. Hatford. "I think Buckman will remember this one for a long, long time."

"Well, let the sale begin!" said Mrs. Hatford, looking around.

"It already has," said Wally.

His mother looked at him. "I thought I told you not to sell anything until we opened at noon."

"Well, we had a little excitement while you were at the game," said Mrs. Larson. "Two women came by and walked off with our prize offering."

"What?" cried Mrs. Hatford.

"Close your eyes," Mrs. Larson said.

Everyone closed their eyes. After a moment, Mrs. Larson said, "Now open." Everyone did.

Mrs. Larson was holding the pair of bloomers against her body. The legs came down almost to her ankles.

"What?" cried Mrs. Hatford and Mrs. Malloy together, while the men only stared.

"These bloomers were made famous by Amelia Bloomer herself!" Mrs. Larson declared, showing them the embroidered label on the inside, and the story had to be told all over again.

At the most dramatic moment, Wally triumphantly held up the picture he had taken of Caroline, sweaty and red-faced, one shoelace untied, with her dress hiked up to her waist and the long muslin bloomers below. Caroline tried to grab the picture away, but Wally held it just out of reach.

"Caroline, you look ravishing!" Beth joked.

Another woman arrived from the auxiliary with a basket of sandwiches for all the helpers, and while they ate, Jenny Bloomer talked some more about her cousins.

"I wondered why they called me and were so anxious to know if I still had all of Mother's things. They asked if I had given away any old photographs, and I said I had—that I had already taken the sale items to the Hatfords—and I guess that's when the trouble began. If they had been honest with me and told me about the letter, I would have shared whatever was inside the picture frame. Instead, they must have come to Buckman, rented a room, and tried every way they could to get that picture without my knowing. I don't think they deserve those bloomers, do you?"

"I think they belong to you, Jenny," said Mrs. Hatford. "And you may do whatever you like with them."

"In that case, I would like to donate them to the museum here in Buckman," said Jenny. "If my cousins show up, we will gladly refund their money, provided they return the photograph, of course. My guess is they will hightail it out of Buckman and the auxiliary will keep the twenty. We can certainly put it to good use at the fire department."

The Hatfords and the Malloys spent the afternoon helping out at the sale. Jake and Josh put customers' purchases in bags for them, Eddie helped carry things out to cars, Beth and her mother made change, Mr. Hatford and Coach Malloy kept their eyes on the customers to see that nothing else was taken, and Wally and Caroline kept one eye out for the two cousins of Jenny Bloomer, but they did not come back. They were probably already on the road, far out of town.

When the sale was over, the tables dismantled, and the leftover items taken away in a pickup truck, the four Hatford boys and the three Malloy girls sat down on the back steps of the Hatford house. Josh and Jake and Peter were still laughing at the photo Wally had taken of Caroline.

"Please give it to me, Wally," Caroline begged.

"Yeah? You want to trade?" asked Jake. "Don't you have some pictures of us?"

"Not on your life!" said Eddie. "You think we should turn over all those pictures of you for only one in return?"

Wally looked quickly at Caroline. Was this the way it was going to be? He wouldn't get those pictures back after all?

"So what else do you want?" asked Josh.

Beth looked at Eddie and Eddie looked at Caroline.

"Quit calling us the Whomper, the Weirdo, and the

Crazie," said Beth, and Eddie nodded. "But it's still not an even trade."

"Well, you'd better make up your mind, because we just might send Caroline's picture to the newspaper. They might like to print it along with the story of how Amelia Bloomer's bloomers got to be in the Buckman Museum," Jake said.

Wally grinned at Caroline, satisfied that for once the boys had the upper hand. But his face fell when Caroline suddenly brightened and said, "Oh, *would* you? *Please?* I'd love to have that picture in the paper. Maybe a talent scout will see it and he'll be looking for someone to play the part of an old-fashioned girl in the eighteen hundreds who has to work in a garment factory, and she steals the bloomers she's been sewing all week to buy food for her little sisters and—"

"Forget it," said Wally. Caroline *wanted* her picture shown around. Caroline *liked* to be seen in bloomers. Caroline was nuts. Caroline was Caroline. He gave up. "For you," he said, and handed her the picture.

The girls looked at him, then at each other.

"You won't call us the Whomper, the Weirdo, and the Crazie anymore?" asked Eddie.

"No," said Josh.

"Deal?"

"Deal." They all put their hands together, one on top of the other, and Eddie went home and returned with the photo album.

"For you," she said, and handed it to Jake.

Jake leafed through the pages quickly to see if all the pictures were there.

This was a little too easy! Wally thought. "How do we know you haven't shown them to people already?" he asked.

"Well, we haven't," said Eddie. "You'll just have to trust us."

"How do we know you haven't made copies and aren't still planning to blackmail us?" asked Josh.

"We aren't," said Beth.

"How do we know you won't go around *telling* people about them?" asked Wally.

"You don't," said Caroline. "So I guess you'll just have to stay on your best behavior."

"Uh . . . not so fast," said Jake. "Maybe *you'll* have to stay on *your* best behavior too!" With that, he pulled something out of his back pocket. "Unless you want these strung up the flagpole at school on Monday."

"What *is* it?" asked Caroline, staring as Jake unfolded it.

"*More* bloomers!" chortled Peter. "Eddie's underpants!"

The Malloy girls stared in horror. Eddie's cheeks turned from pale peach to rosy pink to tomato red.

"Let's play ball!" yelped Josh, pointing to the lines of print going this way and that all over the fabric.

"They're . . . full of holes!" gasped Beth. "Where did you get those?"

"I guess Peter thought they were a dishcloth when

you invited him to stay at your house for dinner," said Wally.

Eddie covered her face in humiliation. "I wish Mother wouldn't use our stuff!" she wailed.

"Okay," said Caroline. "What do we have to do to get them back?"

Wally and his brothers exchanged satisfied smiles. Oh, life was sweet, Wally decided. Life, for a change, was wonderful.

"Well," said Josh, "I suppose you could scrub our toilets for a week, make our beds, and clean out our closets."

The girls could only stare.

"Or maybe you could bow down when you see us coming and call us lord and master," said Jake.

"Never!" said Eddie.

"Or bake us cookies!" said Peter hopefully.

"How about this?" said Wally. "We give them back, but if you ever breathe one word about the pictures in that album, we'll tell everyone we know about Eddie's underpants with all the holes and the *Let's play ball!* messages on them."

"We promise we won't!" said the three Malloy girls together.

"But if *you* go around telling about the underpants, we get to tell about the pictures," said Beth. "Understood?"

"Okay," said Jake and Josh and Wally and Peter.

With that, Jake whirled the underpants once again,

but this time Eddie caught them. And as the girls headed home, Wally heard Eddie say, "Mom won't get any more of *these* for her rag bag, that's for sure!"

"Hey! Good game, Eddie!" Jake called after her.

"You didn't play so bad yourself," said Eddie.

■ ■ ■ ■ ■ ■ ■ ■ ■ ■

Twenty

■

Dear Bill . . .

Dear Bill (and Danny and Steve and Tony and Doug):

Well, we got the pictures back. I don't think the girls are going to tell anyone about them, because we have some blackmail material of our own if they do. (And wouldn't you just like to know what!) Sorry, we can't tell, but man, did we ever luck out!

Not only that, but the Buckman Badgers won the championship. I could hear the cheering from way back here at the house. They say Eddie hit a scorching double in the eighth inning that brought home two runs and won the game. Then, with Jake pitching, Grafton didn't get a single hit in the ninth.

I wasn't at the game, though, and you know why: the Women's Auxiliary yard sale. But we had plenty of excitement of our own. Two women walked off with a framed photograph even after I said the sale hadn't started yet. But I told Caroline to follow them and bring back whatever she could. Well, she did, and you will never guess what was sealed behind the paper on the back of the frame. A pair of underpants! Yep! In case you don't know who Amelia Bloomer was—and these underpants are called bloomers—go to the encyclopedia and look her up.

We still don't know if the Malloys are going back to Ohio or not, but they'll be here for the next few months anyway. We might take them up Indian Knob, or show them the old coal mine.

Right now things are going pretty good, but maybe it's time we found out who really belongs here in Buckman—the Hatfords or the Malloys. Just in case you guys come back, I mean, and the Malloys stay. Just in case they think they can boss us around. I don't mean we'd be enemies or anything. But Caroline always wants to be queen of something, and she just might decide she wants to be queen of us.

Anyway, best wishes from Buckman's winning Badgers and Amelia Bloomer's bloomers.

Wally (and Jake and Josh and Peter)

About the Author

Readers of Phyllis Reynolds Naylor's boys-versus-girls books often want to know who's finally going to win the war. Well, says Naylor, she herself is a girl, but she raised two sons, so she knows how boys feel as well. Readers will just have to wait to see what the Hatfords and the Malloys have in mind.

The town of Buckman in the stories is really Buckhannon, West Virginia, where Naylor's husband spent most of his growing-up years.

Phyllis Reynolds Naylor is the author of more than a hundred books, including the Newbery Award–winning *Shiloh* and the other two books in the Shiloh trilogy, *Shiloh Season* and *Saving Shiloh*. She and her husband live in Bethesda, Maryland. They are the parents of two grown sons and have three grandchildren.